GW00733358

Spectre of Destiny

BOOK 1

J.T.MATHER

Karadas: The Veiled Realm
Spectre of Destiny
First edition
ISBN: 978-1-8380648-0-8 (Paperback)

First published in Great Britain 2022

Edited by David Hambling
The Joy of Pages
www.thejoyofpages.co.uk

Cover illustration by Alex Fusea
www.artstation.com/alexandrufusea

© Map created by J. T. Mather
Book design by J. T. Mather

www.jtmather.com

There is so much more to the world.

All you have to do is close your eyes and imagine it.

J.T.MATHER

Spectre of Destiny is the first of two books in a brand new fantasy series, **Karadas: The Veiled Realm.**

The story begins in April, 1912, somewhere out in the Atlantic Ocean.

While modern mankind believe they have mapped every mountain and sailed every wave on the planet, Theodore Reed soon discovers this be an oversight.

As he sets out on his perilous adventure, he quickly comes to realise that the realm of Karadas is like no other place on Earth.

Explore Karadas in more detail and full colour at **www.jtmather.com/karadas**

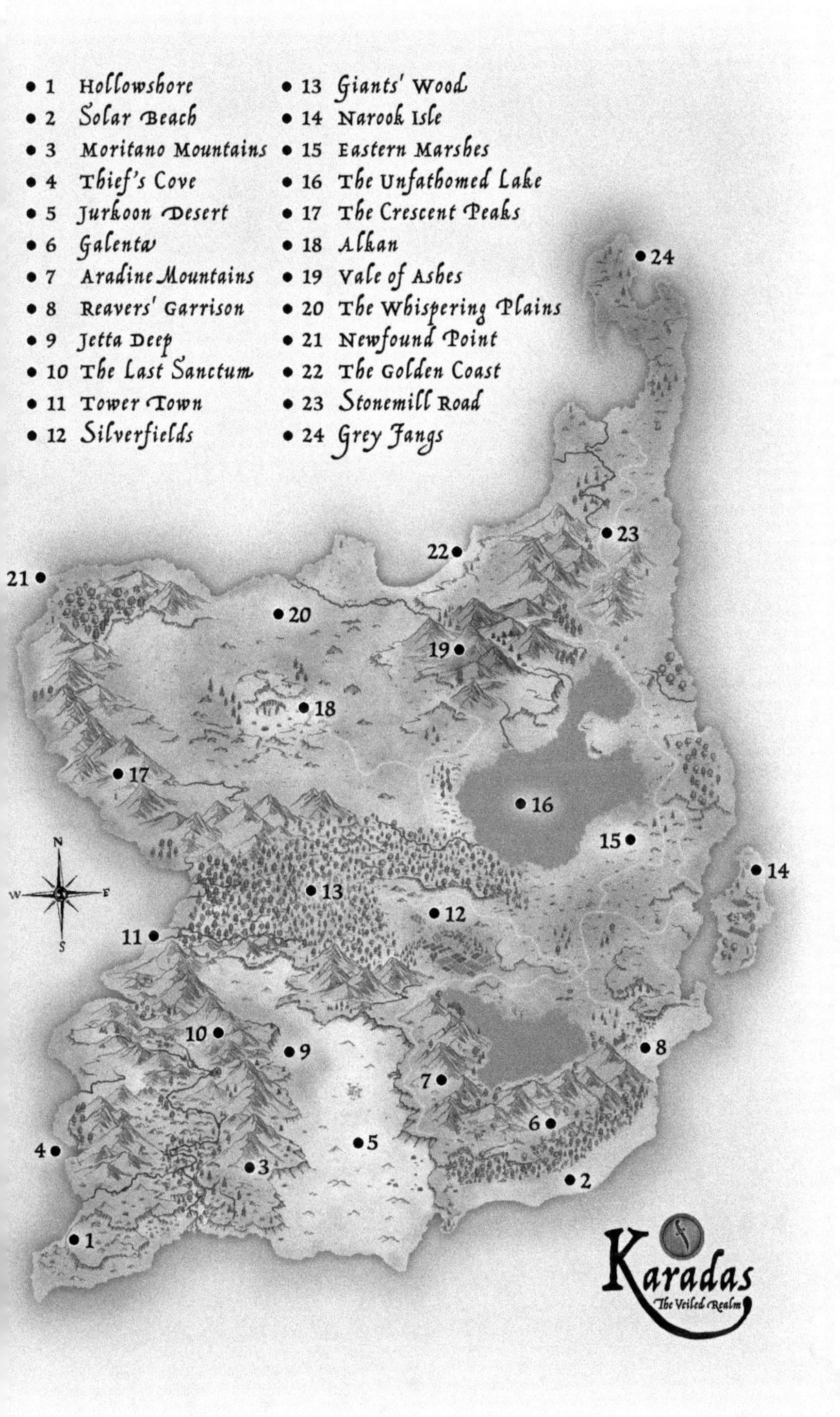

1 Hollowshore
2 Solar Beach
3 Moritano Mountains
4 Thief's Cove
5 Jurkoon Desert
6 Galenta
7 Aradine Mountains
8 Reavers' Garrison
9 Jetta Deep
10 The Last Sanctum
11 Tower Town
12 Silverfields
13 Giants' Wood
14 Narook Isle
15 Eastern Marshes
16 The Unfathomed Lake
17 The Crescent Peaks
18 Alkan
19 Vale of Ashes
20 The Whispering Plains
21 Newfound Point
22 The Golden Coast
23 Stonemill Road
24 Grey Fangs
N
W
E
S
Karadas
The Veiled Realm

Spectre of Destiny

Part 1

Far from home

Part 1 • Chapter 1

Trials of the ocean

April 16th, 1912

Lightning cracked the sky and thunder rolled through the swirling darkness above. The rain came down in sheets, lashing the shark's fin as it rose again from the depths like a blunted cleaver to smash hard against the lifeboat, sending white wooden splinters bursting from its once-smooth hull.

Quite why the shark seemed so determined to overturn their boat, Theodore Reed could not have said. Tears welled in his eyes as he knelt at the bow, hacking desperately at the beast with a hefty dock pole, missing with each frantic blow.

His sister remained at the stern, shivering, and clinging to the tiller with two trembling hands. An expression of pure dread spread over her pale, heart-shaped face as the shark returned, only to circle and vanish below the water.

For two hateful days now, the ocean had played a tedious game, dragging and jostling the youngster's lifeboat up waves the height of church spires and into rifts so deep that the world turned black. Minnie and her older brother had seen nothing but sea and sky in all of that time, light and then dark, nothing more. They had never felt so threatened or vulnerable, so very alone.

"It's gone," Theodore called through the rain. "The shark's gone. It won't come back. I promise, Minnie. I promise." Thunder boomed and lightning lit up the night sky, turning it momentarily into day. *Not like this,* he pleaded silently. *Please, don't let it end like this.*

***

April 14th, 1912

They were two ordinary siblings bound for a new life; two ordinary siblings longing each and every day for their old one. But that could never be. Their misfortune had begun in innocence: a late evening of chasing and hiding from gleeful boys aboard the Titanic, an immense steel ship en route from England to America.

"You children shouldn't be up here," a stern voice called from the stairwell. They glimpsed the white of his beard; it could have been Captain Smith, but none of the children dared to stop and check. A dozen well-dressed boys and one fed-up girl scattered in all directions like cockroaches beyond the pantry door.

Theodore and Minnie ran hand-in-hand across the polished slats of the upper deck, charging up and down stairs and past windows clouded with cigar smoke. They darted between gentlemen dressed in their evening finery and ladies in long vivid gowns, clutching embodied bags and strolling along the deck in silent satin slippers, giggling at the latest quip their partner offered.

In the shadow of a towering smokestack, the siblings crept back up to the boat deck, tiptoeing under a row of round brass lamps that flickered in the dark like fireflies. Theodore led his sister to his latest, daring hiding place, well away from the other passengers. Having explored almost every inch of the ship permitted to him—and many areas that clearly were not—he had found the perfect place for the two of them to hide.

Theodore peaked out. "They'll never find us in here," he said jubilantly. "The other boys are all terrible at this game. Robin's the worst; he'd struggle to find the hand at the end of his own arm!"

"It's a stupid game, Theo," Minnie groaned, rolling her eyes. "A pointless game for silly boys. We'll get in trouble.

Aunt Cordelia… she'll be furious if she finds out we're in here. Please, Theo, I don't like it. The band… they're starting." *I hope they play the David's City song,* she thought to herself. *Father liked that song.* "Right, that's it! I'm going. I want to watch the band play."

"Wait… keep quiet, Min. Someone's coming. Get down."

The pair fell silent, concealed under the tarpaulin of a sizeable lifeboat. Footsteps approached—the booted feet of the ship's crew—ready to carry out their final inspections of the day. Idle chatter wafted in through the gaps of the tarpaulin on breath thick with brandy and damp cigarettes. The second officer oversaw the muster drill with half-hearted instruction, completely unaware of the hidden children. The curly moustache on his upper lip twitched with each command he called out.

Inch by inch, the lifeboat swung out over the side of the ship on sturdy ropes in a chilly breeze. Tonight, though, the drill failed. By error, reckless behaviour, or sheer rotten luck, the crew allowed the lifeboat to come untethered and plummet down to the ocean with the groan and screech of straining metal and rope.

While each of the men pleaded their innocence and argued with one another, the boat drifted steadily away, veiled under a ghostly swirl of evening mist. Over an hour went by before the children's disappearance came to light. By then, the lifeboat, thought to be empty, was nowhere to be seen; carried away on the waves, deeper and deeper into the vast Atlantic Ocean.

***

Night-time came swiftly, just as it had the previous day; their second since the calamity on the steel ship. Alone on the ocean, hungry, thirsty, and petrified of what lay beneath the waves, the young siblings now found themselves in immediate and terrible danger. Any luck that remained with the children—a boy of thirteen and a girl of twelve—had run dangerously low.

Lightning flashed across the sky like white veins as the shark emerged for a fifth time; a monstrous creature in mottled grey skin, criss-crossed with the scars of countless deep-sea battles.

Minnie sat rigid, overwhelmed by fear. It was all she could do to point a rain-soaked finger, hardly able to form any words inside her dry, pinched throat. "Theo. Theo, over there," she squeaked.

"I see it. Get down, Minnie... hold on to something." Theodore clenched his jaw firmly and launched the dock pole. His aim was shaky, and he almost tumbled overboard in his effort, but it was a fine throw. The steel hook tore through the shark's fin to leave a deep gouge. "Got you... I got you!" he jeered through gritted teeth. Any pain the monster may have suffered, it veiled expertly.

"Why is it attacking us?" Minnie sobbed. *I hate it. I*

hate it. Leave us alone!

"The storm… maybe the storm sent it mad. It's gone now… it won't come back." Even he didn't believe the words. Somehow, he had to keep their spirits from sinking beneath the waves. The situation, in reality, seemed hopeless.

A thunder clap ripped through the air as they crouched low in the boat, sheltering as best they could from the rain and wind that seemed to grow fiercer by the hour. Both shivered uncontrollably. Their precious store of woollen blankets lay in a sodden, grey heap at the bottom of the boat, and the meagre cover offered by the tarpaulin had disappeared some time ago, whipped away by a sharp blast of wind to vanish into the night.

Heavy rain rattled the hull and another great boom rang out, and then another. It was a veritable sailor's storm, mighty and ferocious, the kind a boastful captain would recall time and again to gullible young deck hands beside a crackling log fire in the corner of a shady tavern at a wind-swept port.

"I'm sorry, Min," Theodore mumbled. He held up an arm to shield his eyes from the downpour. "The crew, they'll find us. I promise they'll find us. It won't be long. I'm sure we're not too far from the ship."

His sister didn't seem entirely convinced. "You promise?" Strands of wet red hair clung to her face and shoulders. "It's been such a long time. What if we're stranded in this boat forever?"

"Don't worry, they'll be here soon, you'll see. I double promise. And we'll *never* play that stupid hide and seek game ever again! Never, ever!"

Minnie let her eyes close, half laughing, half crying, breathing in the sour reek of kelp wafting on the air. She felt safer in her brother's arms. *I never did like that game,* she told herself. *Theo's right, they'll find us soon. The entire crew must have joined the search by now, every single one of them.*

Their peaceful moment ended as the shark returned to ram the hull, despite her brother's promise. Wood and water exploded into the air and the crunch of timber rang in their ears.

The collision knocked Minnie to the bottom of the boat and on to the sopping wet blanket pile. In a moment of desperation, her hands seized the heavy handle of an oar, and with all the strength left in her stick-thin arms, she jabbed at the beast's lidless eye through a wide crack in the hull. It was enough, though, and there was no hiding the pain this time. The shark thrashed in agony, pounding the boat with the flat of an enormous tail before sinking beneath the waves.

Seawater seeped into the lifeboat at an alarming rate, gushing in through multiple splits in the ruined hull. The children cowered together on a low bench at the stern, soaked and weary, gripped by panic.

Theodore tightened the drawstrings of his sister's life jacket before fastening his own. "Be brave, Minnie," he yelled, forcing their only lifebuoy into her hands. "Keep this close. I promise we'll be safe, nothing will..."

A gigantic wave cut short his comforting words, engulfing the boat with the force of a hammer striking an anvil. Theodore floundered between the slats with his plimsoles sliding uselessly against the wet wood. Both hands reached for Minnie, but neither found her. His sister, his sweet young sister, had vanished, swept away into the churning ocean, lost in the blinding dark.

"Minnie!" he screamed. He circled the boat, scanning the water through eyes filled with salt and tears and dismay, calling out into the unrelenting storm that simply would not end. "Minnie, come back! Where are you? Come back! Please come back. Minnie..." *I can't lose you,* his mind cried in agony. *Not you, Min... not you. You're all I have left!*

Wave after wave swept on to the crippled boat, pounding Theodore's body and squeezing the breath from his lungs. Seawater surged over the top of him once, twice, and then a third time as the ocean claimed its prize. In seconds, the waves had swallowed the lifeboat whole, drawing it down into a murky abyss.

Overwhelmed and afraid, Theodore struggled to keep afloat. Any hope that remained—his very survival—was now entrusted to the lifejacket strapped to his chest.

Part 1 • Chapter 2

This uncharted coast

Theodore lay spread-eagled on a vast, deserted beach, alone, but alive. Drizzle swept over his body from the grey sky as a band of gnarly white crabs nibbled at the fingers of his outstretched hand. He awoke with a jolt and staggered to his feet on unsteady legs, barking up a flurry of deep coughs and shaking away the pincers clinging to his skin. "Get away. Get back... leave me alone!"

Furious at the disturbance, the crabs came at him screeching and scuttling in a sideways melee, eager to latch back on to the boy's soft skin. They were ravenous and outnumbered him at least twenty to one.

"Get back!" Theodore dashed through the rain and across the sand, only daring to slow when the crab army was almost out of sight—barely pale specks along the shore. *Where on earth am I?* he thought. *What is this place?*

Once his breathing settled and the pounding of his heart calmed a little, Theodore let his life jacket drop to the ground in a soggy heap. He brushed the black hair away from his dark blue eyes with a shaky hand to look all around.

Huge, frothing waves rolled between the craggy rocks just out to sea and on to the sand, one after the next to send great plumes of salt spray tumbling through the air. A thick jungle grew at his back—a wall of trees and leaves in countless shades of green and brown, red and copper, running for miles along the coast in either direction.

His attention settled on a jagged black pillar half-buried in the sand close by. It stood tall and glossy, and on touching the stone, the pillar shimmered with a peculiar beauty. Silver veins pulsed just under the surface where the dull, warped reflection of a boy looked back. *So strange.* A memory of flint arrowheads popped unexpectedly into Theodore's mind. While he had taken only a pocket of conkers to school for his end-of-term display, another pupil had presented a glass case containing his grandfather's collection of arrowheads from all across the world.

This was certainly no arrowhead. The pillar standing before him was very different; ominous, and over twice the height of a man. He could see more up and down the coast, embedded in the sand between knots of coral weed and runnels of rainwater trickling down the beach toward the ocean. Most stood straight while a handful leant sleepily to one side. "Am I dreaming this? Where on earth am I?"

The seashore curved inward further along where a large section of the jungle lay decimated; palm trees reduced to ragged strips of splintered wood and fractured stumps, wreathed in twisting red vines. Theodore shuffled forward to peer through the gap. He could see towering cliffs rising above the trees in the distance like a row of tombstones among a field of unkempt weeds, and mountain peaks further back, tall and grey, reaching up to caress the long bands of charcoal cloud drifting by.

Thoughts of the stricken lifeboat flashed suddenly back into his mind, thoughts that snapped immediately to his sister. "Min? Minnie, are you here?" he called out, barely able to hear his own voice above the thump and roar of waves hammering the shore. "Where are you?" *I promised her. I promised she'd be safe.*

Desperate to find his sister—and fearful he may not—Theodore jogged along the beach with his head down, scanning the sand, searching for a glimmer of hope; a footprint, a bootlace, anything. *Please, Min. Please be safe.* The smash and rumble of breaking waves accompanied his every step, and the jungle watched on through a pale haze, dark and brooding, unwilling to offer any help even if it could.

On he trekked, calling Minnie's name repeatedly, but no reply came back. All he heard were the waves. *She's not here,* he thought glumly. *Where is she?* The rain thinned after a while and in its place, a light morning mist rolled in off the ocean. Birds emerged from hidden nests and shelters throughout the jungle to twitter, hoot, and squawk among the treetops. He watched a flock of scrawny waders drift down on threadbare wings to probe at the sand, tottering around on lanky pink legs.

Theodore trudged beside the waves dressed in sodden canvas plimsoles, sagging wool trousers, and a once-cream shirt. A lilac silk waistcoat flapped limply at his chest like a flag caught in the wind, held loosely by a single, valiant button. In the few months he and Minnie had known their new guardian, Aunt Cordelia, she had always made the children dress to perfection, never allowing them to appear as an embarrassment in front of her lavish, so-called friends. If Cordelia could see him now, as a vagrant, she would punish him for sure, though it never took much for either sibling to receive a scolding from their spiteful aunt.

His attention peaked immediately at the sight of an object lurching and whirling in the surf up ahead. Ripples of trepidation arose in his stomach. "The lifeboat!" Theodore cried out. Only part of the boat now remained, caught in the tide and nudging up against the shore. A painted red flag adorned the bow, as did a white metal nameplate. In black text, it simply read, S.S. Titanic.

"Minnie!" Even from a distance, it was clear he would not find his sister amongst the wreckage. He remembered it all so clearly now, the storm and the potent waves that had swept her away and into the ocean. Theodore stood for a while, waist-deep in the surf, wishing he possessed an ability to change the past or a power to save those he had loved and lost. So many already. Too many.

He clambered over the hull in a sullen mood to discover a half-filled water canister hidden under a sad, torn life jacket. "That's where you were," he mumbled. The only other canister the pair had shared ran dry long ago. It was most likely on the ocean bed by now. Even so, he drank deeply and wiped his mouth. At that moment, a vivid object caught his eye, half buried in the silt among a school of translucent shrimp. "Minnie's rainbow bracelet."

It had been his gift to his sister on her twelfth birthday, not three weeks past, with each wooden bead painted a different colour. Theodore scooped up the bracelet and held it tight. *She must be alive,* he told himself. *She must be.* He stood in a daze before the glittery waves, with a fiery determination swelling inside his chest, burning brighter than ever. *I have to find her; I have to. She's all I have left.*

A muffled thud broke his trance. Matted sand and

shingle quivered all around as another thud landed, louder this time, deeper. And then it emerged. Theodore's mouth fell open as a gruesome creature lumbered across the sand further up the coast, appearing steadily through a swirl of light, white mist. It was terrible to behold. A beast from a half-forgotten myth, a demonic monster from a harrowing, dark dream. *This can't be real? This must be a nightmare.*

The creature trudged upright on two stumpy legs as thick as tree trunks, kicking at the sand with a cloven hoof, looking to unearth a hidden morsel. Rust-coloured scales covered its stooped, heavy-set body, thick shoulders and squat neck and back. Even from a distance, he could see its dry lipless mouth, crammed with needle-sharp teeth, perfect for stripping the flesh from living prey.

Theodore cowered behind the half-boat, edging back into the water. "It's coming closer. What do I do?" he whispered, hoping a voice would guide him to safety. None did. His body trembled and blood pumped cold through his veins, colder than the waves sloshing against his body.

His eyes followed the beast over the rim of the hull, watching a pair of tiny orange birds dart between its craggy scales in search of parasites. After digging again at the beach, the monster turned in a ponderous circle to stare out over the ocean, blowing a rumbled snort through tight, wet nostrils.

Don't look this way, he begged. *Please don't see me. Go back. Go back!* Time stood still as the beast turned slowly. Dead black eyes in a solid bulbous head blinked as they locked on to the remains of the lifeboat.

Any hope of an escape vanished in that moment. Theodore could hear the beast approaching, panting with a deathly groan, and for a few seconds, he could only squeeze his eyes shut. His mind felt paralysed, unable to muster any notion of what to do. The hull creaked as a long claw probed at the wood, nudging the wreck against his shoulder. *Go now, Theo. You have to go now!*

Theodore drew in three deep breaths and clenched his jaw tight. He sprinted as fast as his legs would carry him over the sand, clutching the water canister and Minnie's bracelet in shaky white fingers. Almost immediately, he stumbled to the ground, betrayed by his own dangling laces. He jumped up, only for a ferocious roar to send him blundering to the sand for a second time. Birds fled from the treetops screeching as another bellow rang out, more terrible than the first.

He struggled to his feet and ran, forcing himself to look ahead, only ahead, to the jungle, every moment fearing a burly, clawed hand would snatch him up. He could not dare to imagine what would happen after that.

Enraged, the monster gave chase. Its two great legs had a sure stride, but the boy was swift. A sizeable gap quickly opened up between the hunter and its escaping prey, but the beast was not done yet. Two gnarled fists struck the beach like stone hammers to send wet sand leaping a foot into the air.

Theodore lost his balance and hit the ground hard. "Get up. Get up!" he screamed at himself. He scrambled forward, plastered head to foot in sand and bits of broken shell to make a last desperate charge for the trees. His lungs strained and his legs ached, but he could not rest, not even for a second. An earthy scent grew more potent with each weary stride. Sharp yellow leaves whipped and mauled his face as he charged deeper and deeper into the shadowy jungle.

Branches cracked, and timber splintered. The beast swiped at the wall of wood and leaf at his back, tearing at the jungle and plucking palm trees from the ground as easily as a toddler might pick a flower.

Theodore cowered amongst the undergrowth, shocked and exhausted and gripped with a fear he had never known before, watching the creature with terrified wide eyes. He crawled inside a hollowed tree stump nearby and curled up into a ball among the clammy grey fungi, clamping both hands over his ears, desperate to block out all sight and sound of the horrific monster.

Eventually, the beast abandoned the hunt. It slashed at the trees and gave a final bellow, furious that a substantial meal of meat and bone had escaped its grasp.

Sweat ran over Theodore's skin like warm rain,

stinging the scratches on his hands and face. His heart felt as though it might burst at any moment. Fatigued, confused and afraid, he wished with every thought to wake up, to discover this entire experience was all just a dark and harrowing nightmare.

Part 1 · Chapter 3

Half a world away

Silence claimed the jungle for a time. Black earth, leaves, and broken branches littered the sand beyond the trees. Huge tree trunks too, torn root and stem from the ground to lay shattered on the beach. Only when the beast had reached a suitably safe distance did the birds dare to return to fill the jungle with their treetop ballad, with unseen frogs and insects adding their own curious tones to the natural orchestra.

With his courage somewhat restored, Theodore wriggled free from the tree stump on mud-stained knees and elbows, crawling across a carpet of moss and over to a damp clay verge, surrounded by untamed plants. He watched a silky grey mouse foraging for seeds and nuts among the roots, but at the sight of the giant boy staring back, she quickly darted away to the safety of her burrow.

"Minnie?" he called meekly into the gloom, fearful his voice may summon back the monster. "Can you hear me?" Doubts festered in his muddled mind. If his sister had somehow survived the storm and made it to land, past that dreadful creature and into the jungle... what other dangers lurked here? Even where he knelt, the plants all around looked wild and fierce, evolved to survive in a harsh and hostile world.

Thoughts lingered, too, of their aunt. She would be outwardly frantic the children had gone missing from the ship. Cordelia would surely weep fake tears. Excessive, thick mascara would stream down her powdered, bony cheeks while she professed to anyone and everyone how much she loved and missed her wonderful niece and handsome nephew. It was his grim suspicion, however, that she would be secretly glad to see the back of them both.

Minnie and Theodore's parents had unexpectedly died less than six months past, a shock that neither had yet to recover from. Cordelia—their late father's sister—had become their guardian, with their grandfather demanding she take on the duty of their upbringing. Aunt Cordelia clearly had neither the appetite nor the character for such a task. She possessed a remarkably short temper and expressed little to no empathy. The children would merely be a nuisance; an inconvenience to her luxurious, selfish lifestyle. Grudgingly, she had agreed. A threat from her own father regarding any inheritance she may receive had helped to sway the decision. And so, the grown-ups had decided, the siblings would move from England to their aunt's home in New York immediately.

His focus flashed back to the present. Theodore plucked the cobwebs from his ruined clothes, mulling over what to do next. Eventually, he decided it would be safest to steer inland, away from the beach and toward the cliffs rising up beyond the jungle. *As far away as possible from that awful creature!*

Although the cliffs looked to be a good few miles away, if he could somehow make it to the top, with an unobstructed view, his chances of finding a coastal town or village would surely increase. Even the sight of a single person would allow him a sliver of hope. *Just one person,* he thought. *Any person.*

It took a few minutes to leaver a sturdy branch from a half-dead tree before Theodore let out a weary sigh and set off through the jungle, hacking at the shoulder-high plants in his path. For some time along the way, he called out his sister's name, desperate for a reply. "Minnie, please be safe." *I'll find you soon, I promise.* Whistles and howls carried through the muggy air, but Minnie's voice remained silent.

Even after an hour or more, his mind could not quite

fathom where in the world this strange place could actually be. *Africa, perhaps. Maybe a Caribbean island? But they're thousands of miles away. We can't have drifted that far.* In days gone by, he and his father had spent many a pleasant hour at home studying paper maps of the world. The jigsaw of countries and skilfully sketched continents had always fascinated them both.

Theodore loved his father's stories, too, especially any concerning the British Empire. And above all, those involving a battle—particularly the battles his own father had fought in abroad under the command of Field Marshal Frederick Roberts, or Bobs, as the men called him. He wondered if his father had ever fought here, in this very jungle. *Wherever it is, it's somewhere far too hot,* he decided finally, *not like England.* Theodore missed England. He missed his father, and his mother, too. Most of all, though, he missed his sister. *Stay safe, Minnie.*

He struggled on, wiping sweat beads from his brow with an already sweat-soaked sleeve. Tangled barbs that would not part and deep, stench-filled bogs forced his direction to change several times. The frustration of it all melted away when a small glade opened out, bathed in the morning sunlight. Theodore rested here for a while, sipping warm water from his dented canister and allowing the sun to sooth his jaded skin.

"Hello?" he called again. A lull settled over the jungle. Theodore's curiosity peaked at the sound of water trickling close by. He trudged through a large patch of marshy black mud and between ferns reaching as high as his shoulders to arrive at a narrow brick duct choked with broken stone, dead leaves, and branches. Every brick had long since cracked and turned a dismal shade of grey-green. The water looked equally bleak. "Maybe this leads to a village?"

The channel ran straight for a quarter mile until it vanished beneath a half-sunken archway at the foot of a ruined stone temple. What remained of the age-old structure looked anything but inviting. Moss and thick creepers covered almost all of the crumbling stonework, with the rest cloaked in shadow.

"What a dreary place," he muttered under his breath, eyeing the window slots up above. The carved stone head of a serpent looked down from the wall, with a forked tongue eroded down to a rounded stump. To Theodore's ears, even the light babble of the brick stream seemed to hiss now rather than trickle.

The eerie temple soon lay far behind. Another hour of drudgery passed by and then another, plodding through undergrowth and over fallen tree trunks that all seemed to look the same. Before long, Theodore changed direction, anxious he had merely walked in a circle. He journeyed deeper into the jungle, up and down greasy mud banks and through rubbery leaves striped with resin. A damp, narrow gully that appeared to be a promising route turned out to be a dead end, and the smell he found there was far from pleasant.

After what felt like an entire day—grazed and riddled with thorn cuts—he eventually arrived at a wide, rocky canyon. The chasm split the jungle clean in two, and on the far side, the cliffs loomed tall in the distance, casting a dark shadow over the trees below. *How will I ever get over there?* If the chasm had a bottom, his eyes could not make it out. He saw only a black void dropping to infinity.

"It must narrow at some point." He pressed on, keeping the canyon to his right. Glossy violet flowers grew in bunches all around, attracting a host of colourful butterflies and tiny red birds, all enticed by the sweet scent of nectar wafting in the air.

Theodore brushed past a tangle of hanging vines and his eyes grew wide at the sight of three timber beams spanning the canyon up ahead. Thin ropes and wooden tacks held the primitive bridge in place, linking two broad ledges jutting out from either side. *People... there must be people here,* he decided. *Someone built this bridge.* Excitement swelled as he took a knee, running his fingers through the fallen leaves and twigs scattered across a narrow, worn track, disappearing back into the jungle behind him. The track continued on towards the cliffs on the far side of the bridge. *Maybe Minnie came this way?*

"Hello... is anyone here?" His voice echoed down into the canyon, as if five other boys had called out alongside him. "Minnie, can you hear me?" Only the echoes replied.

Theodore edged out on to the bridge past a cloud of swirling gnats, keeping his eyes forward, being nowhere near brave enough to look down. The beams bowed and creaked painfully with each nervy step. *Don't look down. Just keep moving.*

"Minnie," he called again in hope. "It's me, Theo. Min, are you..." The crack and split of wood answered him this time. He leapt towards the far ledge like a jumping frog as the bridge gave way beneath his feet. The water canister slipped from his grasp and tumbled into the darkness along with lengths of shattered timber, all clinking and crashing and clattering against the canyon walls on their way down.

Theodore fought with all of his strength to hold on, clinging to the edge. His fingers felt as though they may snap at any moment, and his muddy plimsoles squeaked and scraped against the bare rock, searching for a foothold that refused to appear. He hung from the ledge for what seemed like an age. *I can't hold on.* "Minnie!" *I have to hold on. I have to.* "Help me!" Birds and insects buzzed and chirped and whistled throughout the jungle, though not one of them could offer the boy any help.

His head twisted to one side as a faint scratching noise drifted up from the depths. The eerie sound of scuttling legs grew louder and closer, and closer still, creeping steadily up the canyon walls and into the dim light above. Theodore's heart went to his throat as he spied them—

all of them—a dozen prickly spiders as large as hounds, wrapped in gold crinkled skin. Their many cold eyes shimmered white in the darkness like a hundred deadly stars in a night sky.

Theodore squeezed his eyes tight, overwhelmed with dread and weariness. He had already endured more anguish and distress than most youngsters might face in an entire lifetime, maybe ten lifetimes! The relentless torment seemed absurd and wholly unjust. Yet now it seemed he must face a little more. It would appear that the cruel world had not quite finished with him just yet.

His fingers burned, and his head thumped. The rank stench of the creatures turned his stomach, turning the blood in his veins to ice. Theodore screamed as the first of many barbed legs began jabbing at his ankles, gently at first, casually selecting on a spot to latch on to.

"Get back. Away, get away from me… help!" Theodore thrashed out an exhausted leg, catching an overly confident spider square in the face to send it tumbling to its doom with a horrifying shriek. The futile act seemed to only spur the others on. Working together, the spiders approached from both sides and below, hooking on to the boy's dangling feet and binding his legs in a tacky clear silk as strong as steel wire.

Theodore's energy gradually drained away until none remained to fight back. Repulsive, twitching fangs edged ever closer, snipping and slurping beside his ears, ready to infuse his body with deadly venom. All of his hope faded; he knew his end had surely come. *I'm sorry, Minnie. I'm so sorry.* His fingers slipped down the ledge one after the next, and with a final, painful snap, his grip failed.

But the fall was brief.

His eyes sprung open to see tiny gloved hands seizing his wrists, pulling him up from the infested canyon. A crumb of hope rose inside his chest. Blocks of stone rained down on to the spider horde, yet still they resisted, refusing to give up their prize. Theodore's head was spinning. His body surrendered as the two forces stretched him thin in a terrible tug of war in which he was the rope. Every tendon and joint felt within seconds of tearing apart.

Several spiders rushed up to tackle the stone throwers, desperate to claim the boy for themselves. Shouts and angry shrieks reverberated throughout the jungle as the two groups clashed. Eventually, the spiders began a steady retreat, forced back at spear point. The tide of battle turned further when a hail of arrows whistled into their numbers, splattering and smearing the walls with gloopy grey blood, sending the spiders tumbling into the canyon, limp and broken, one after the next. The few to have survived had no choice but to withdraw back down to their dark, sorrowful lair, wounded, demoralised, and utterly famished.

Theodore's mind was a blur. His arms and shoulders throbbed as they hauled his body up and out of danger.

He couldn't even feel his legs anymore. The battle for his life had left him completely drained. Laid to one side, his mysterious saviours hurried to cut away the tangle of silken bonds. Friend or foe, that was unknown, but as his eyes gently closed, in a last hazy moment, Theodore looked upon a remarkable sight, a sight he could barely believe.

Part 1 • Chapter 4

Galenta

A fresh morning breeze caressed Theodore's face, waking him from sleep. He sat up gingerly, propped up on silk and woollen pillows no larger than handkerchiefs to look out from a tall, angled cave. The walls and peaked ceiling were natural, coarse stone, with a polished floor that gleamed like fine marble. In the distance, his bleary eyes watched a dazzling amber sun rise above the ocean to warm another new day.

He found himself dressed in a soft cotton gown; a gown meant for a far younger child. His own clothes and plimsoles lay close by, cleaned and stitched. Theodore shuffled forward and froze instantly as a gust of wind whipped past the cave to tug at his gown. His fingers gripped the wall and he edging forward to look out over the jungle. "Where on earth am I?" Deep green and blood red leaves twinkled with morning dew down below, and west to east, the beach separated the sea from the jungle like a serpent of rich golden sand. The cave—he realised with newly found respect—was at least two hundred feet above the ground, high up inside a cliff face. *How did I get up here?* Then he remembered the spiders! "They were enormous..."

"Good morning, friend," a well-spoken voice announced from the rear of the cave. "The winds are potent today. Best that you stay clear from the edge; it is a long way to fall." A silhouette appeared from the shadows, gliding across the floor to light a small oil lamp and four stubby candles along the far wall with a white wick.

Theodore gazed at the tiny, humanlike figure. He stood only four feet tall, wearing a silvery gown finished at the neck and sleeves with navy trim. Round, emerald eyes gleamed in a round bronze face, between recessed ears and above a small button nose. Thin white braids grew from the centre of an otherwise hairless scalp, running down his back to brush the thick leather belt at his waist.

Visions of the infested canyon flashed through Theodore's mind; to the heroes who had saved him. *I did see them,* he thought. *They were real. There were little people there!* His eyes hadn't lied after all.

"Welcome," said the tiny man, smiling warmly.

"Who... who are you?" Theodore stuttered. "Where am I? Have you seen my sister, Minnie?"

"Have patience. You have endured a great deal. I am Rhal. It is an honour to meet you. You are quite safe; a most welcome guest here." Rhal peered down to the trees far below. "You are highly fortunate. Few who enter the Wilandro Jungle escape unharmed."

"Unharmed?" said Theodore. "I'm scratched all over, and giant spiders almost had me for dinner. And that thing... that giant monster on the beach... what in all the world was *that?*"

"You encountered Rakista... and you survived?" Rhal nodded in admiration. "My apologies. Fortunate is an insult. Remarkable would be far more appropriate." He snuffed out the wick, bowed low, and disappeared into the shadows at the back of the cave.

Each day stranger than the last. Left alone with the scent of candle wax, Theodore discovered a wicker basket filled with bite-size fruit wrapped in red vines, along with warm bread cakes sprinkled with nuts and berries. He ate gratefully, his belly groaning with pleasure. After that, he enjoyed a jar of sweet honey-flavoured drink. The clay goblet provided was so minute, it took six cups to quench his considerable thirst.

The coast below lay bathed in morning sunlight. Theodore looked out from the cave, twiddling the rainbow bracelet at his wrist. Uneasy thoughts of his missing sister turned through his mind. *I know you're alive. I can feel it,* he told himself. *Stay safe, Minnie, I promise I'll find you.* He pondered again just where in the world this place could be. The fierce creatures and harsh landscape were unlike anything he had seen or read about. In particular, the monster on the sand—Rakista. Even the very name gave rise to a shiver.

Time passed, drifting between sleep and deep thought. He awoke to the faint sound of distant music and song and quickly pulled on his own clothes—minus Aunt Cordelia's vulgar lilac waist coat. Theodore followed the sound of harps and drums through a narrow, sparsely lit corridor, around twists and turns in the rock. The melody grew louder and closer until he emerged into the light.

Theodore's mouth fell open. He gazed around in wonder, with the tranquil music only adding to the breathtaking scene. "It's a city," he whispered to himself. "What is this place?"

It was extraordinary to look upon; an entire city carved into a deep, circular basin under the shadow of the mountains. Hundreds of tiny wooden doors and windows, aisles, and walkways covered the steep, slanting walls, and above even these, a dozen round turrets with mossy thatched roofs hugged the rocks, rising into a perfect afternoon sky. Wisps of peculiar yellow smoke wafted from chimneys and vents into the air, where he could see snow-white birds soaring on the breeze. At the far edge of the incredible city, a clear waterfall, twelve feet wide, flowed from high above. Theodore was utterly astounded. He had seen nothing like it. So unusual. So incredible.

Horns and drums reached a crescendo to bring Theodore's attention back to where he stood. Rhal, the silver-robed figure he had met earlier, waited patiently on a long timber balcony to his right. He raised a tiny hand, and the music faded. Only a trio of wooden flutes continued to play.

An excited crowd of chest-high folk—and even smaller children—had gathered on an oval lawn close by. All had bright emerald eyes and wore exquisite outfits. There were tiny females in oyster silk, bone grey lace and rich velvet flecked with coloured sequins. White braided hair fell forward in thick locks over their narrow shoulders. Slightly larger males donned cream linen and tanned black leather, with a single plait of white hair hanging at their back. The rumble of the waterfall grew louder as the crowd gradually fell silent.

"Welcome," Rhal announced. "It is a joy to have you here." His voice resonated across the lawn. Theodore raised an eyebrow, speechless and mystified in equal measure. "Apologies, my friend. Forgive my manners. We are the Borini, and you stand now in Galenta, our fine and free city."

A cheer went up from the crowd. Calls and claps of jubilation rang out.

"I speak on behalf of our Queen, our consul. She is keen to meet you." Rhal clapped three times, directed the Borini folk to move aside.

Theodore had little choice but to allow the chattering crowd to steer him through the narrow twisting streets, past tiny carved doors and under high stone arches clad with white ivy, along torch-lit passages blackened by soot and over a wide timber bridge crowded with workshops and tall, crooked houses, each three or four stories high. Everything he looked upon had been constructed to cater for the Borini's smaller stature.

Youngsters gaped at the boy as they worked butter churns, and far older Borini stopped whittling sticks to stare, chuffing on long curved pipes that drooped down from their mouths. Even the bearded goats walking in circles to power an immense wooden mill wheel paused at the sight of their exceedingly strange guest.

A troop of stern-looking soldiers dressed in burgundy canvas and studded leather stood to attention up ahead, both male and female. Silk banners fluttered above their heads, portraying a white hawk in flight, set on a dark green background. Other soldiers straddled shiny black beetles as large as well-fed hogs, somehow enhanced to an incredible size. Each possessed razor-sharp, powerful mandibles, and—to Theodore—appeared similar to the stag beetles he would often find scurrying around the meadows back home. Unlike the others, the largest beetle at the head of the group displayed a large jutting horn to further elevate its fierce appearance.

On and on they walked toward the magnificent waterfall, flanked by the soldiers and their beasts. Young Borini girls and boys danced in the boy's shadow as the procession halted beside a circular pool clad in coral, jade and warm ruby tiles. Trumpets and slow drums beckoned the soldiers into position around the pool where the waterfall sparkled in the morning sun.

Theodore gasped as the waterfall separated into two huge drapes, filling the air with a fine mist that clung pleasantly to his skin. Polished stone blocks came next, rising from the water to create a walkway over the strangely still pool, leading into a hidden tunnel. A solid gold door stood sealed in the darkness beyond.

"Follow, my friend," said Rhal, who had appeared by his side.

"In there?" Theodore yelled. He could barely hear his own voice over the din of the water. His heart thumped. Still, he entered regardless, ducking low to avoid a timber beam embedded in the ceiling. "Where are you taking me?"

Rhal knocked twice on the golden door with a short oak staff. "To the royal chamber. Our Queen awaits." The door promptly swung open.

A sloping walkway led down into a large, round hall,

and all sounds from the waterfall faded. Theodore's body relaxed a touch as he breathed in the welcome fragrances of spice and peppermint in the air. His anxiety and fear evaporated further when he heard a wondrous, tender voice singing in unknown words from an unseen balcony above. *I wonder what this song is about?* he thought. *It's beautiful.*

Four round slots in a peaked ceiling allowed the sunlight to shine down, catching on the silver, gold, and regal stones twinkling brightly all around. At the centre of the room, the Queen of the Borini stood patiently beside a glowing blue pool with an elegant silver band resting upon her hairless head. She wore a spotless ice white gown, and a single amber gem hung at her neck.

Theodore followed Rhal's example by bowing to the Queen. Two hooded guards stood to attention in the shadows behind her like sculpted stone figures. Only the light from a heavy iron brazier between them gave any hint that they were even there.

"Come. It would honour me if you would sit," said the Queen in an alluring, soft voice. Her emerald eyes glinted. "I have many questions. What would we name our human guest?"

Theodore blushed and bowed a second time. "Thank you." He sat cross-legged beside the pool, gazing into the water. "My name's Theodore... Theodore Reed. I'm so confused, this place..."

"All in good time, Master Reed," Rhal whispered. "You are safe here."

The Queen settled on a wicker throne, intertwined with red and white ribbons. "Please, you must tell me how you came to be here."

Where to begin! Theodore let out a sigh, ready to detail his dreadful account of the previous few days, every part of it. In turn, he listened with fascination for what seemed like hours, captivated by the Queen's sweet, agreeable tone. She named the realm Karadas. A land of unequalled beauty, able to repel the bitter chill of the ocean winds. *This is incredible. It can't be true... can it?*

"But where is Karadas?" Theodore asked, still quite baffled by the whole experience. "I've seen lots of maps, even a globe once, but I've never heard of a place called Karadas."

"Your world is vast and full of danger," said the Queen. "Working together long ago, beings of remarkable knowledge, the Guardians of Zell-Ku and the Warlocks of Karadas, created a powerful shroud over our land; a cloak of invisibility to veil the entire realm."

Rhal spoke this time, clearing his throat. "The Guardians placed pillars of obsidian all around the coast. Receptacles, if you like. Blessed with potent magic, their energy conceals us from the outside world."

The stones on the beach, Theodore recalled, *the giant arrowheads.* "Magic? But magic doesn't really exist. Does it?"

The Queen smiled. "Tell me, how would *you* explain it,

Theodore Reed?"

"So, humans don't know about this place? They don't even realise Karadas exists?"

"Humankind, for now, is unaware of Karadas," Rhal answered. "As far as we are aware, you are the first human visitor to come here in many years. Men arrived long ago in great timber ships, hurling black rocks that shattered the land and boomed as loud as fury."

Pirates, they must have been pirates. Theodore's father had often told him and his sister tales of pirates by the fireside when they were young. Minnie had never believed much of it; just another story dreamed up to frighten children.

"Reavers came here to plunder, but their quest would eventually end in ruin," Rhal continued. "The waves that encircle our land smashed their boats into splinters. It is impossible to leave Karadas by way of the ocean."

"So, Karadas is an island?"

"Islands are small, my friend. Karadas is vast. But the ocean flows all around, that much is true." he pushed his shoulders back, proud of the revelation.

Bright white lanterns sparked to life to replace the fading sunlight, and servants arrived soon after bearing food and drinks: fresh bowls of seafood broth, long breads coated with sweet preserve, dates and olives, and even a tray of edible pink petals. While the three enjoyed their meal, Theodore's thoughts shifted to his sister. An expression of pure joy spread over his face at Rhal's glorious news: Minnie was alive, discovered along the coast the night before last.

"She's alive! She survived the storm." Theodore laughed and clapped his hands. His blue eyes glistened with tears. "I *knew* she was alive; Minnie's much stronger than she looks. Where is she? I need to see her."

His mood swiftly altered to one of anger and frustration. Although a company of Borini scouts had indeed set eyes on his sister, they had arrived too late to whisk her away. Instead, a hateful race of soulless creatures from the north—the Vorath—had already bundled her into a wooden box cart. The Vorath would put Minnie to work in the fields, or mines… or something worse. She would join a host of other ill-fated folk seized throughout Karadas as a slave in the Vorath's service.

"The Borini have remained hidden from strife for two generations," said the Queen. "To interfere would jeopardise our safety. I am sorry, Theodore Reed, but we could do nothing."

"We have to go after her!" Theodore cried. He jumped up and clenched his fists. "She's my sister, my only family. If we go now, I can fight…"

"You would not catch them, my dear." The Queen spoke with a gentle tone, leaning back into her throne. "Already they are a day's ride ahead, at least."

Theodore looked stern. The Queen remained calm. "I

won't leave her. I'll go alone if I have to."

The Queen sat, shaking her head. "It is an impossible task, my dear. I wish it were otherwise."

"You're wrong," Theodore said, too sharply. "There *is* hope. I still have hope." *Cowards, they're all afraid,* he fumed. *I'll save you, Minnie, I promise I'll save you.* Tears of joy had turned to bitter blotches around his eyes. He stormed from the royal chamber, beyond the waterfall, and out into the narrow lamplit streets.

"Theodore Reed shall return," the Queen reassured Rhal. "There is something about him… I have a sense for this boy. We must remain patient."

Rhal's usual smile was absent as he bowed, leaving the Queen alone to enjoy the pink petals she seemed so fond of.

Karadas was an uncharted land and danger would surely lurk at every turn, but Theodore would not—no, he could not—leave Minnie to these vile creatures. With his last breath, he would find and free her. Then, together, the siblings would somehow discover a way to escape this perilous land forever.

Part 1 • Chapter 5

The welcome stranger

As much as he tried, Theodore could not make out the words to the song. It came as a muffled sound to his ears. Two young girls played hopscotch in the farmyard, skipping from one chalk square to the next. The vision was cloudy. *Is that Ruth and Rosie, the Downing children... Am I back home? Am I back in Corsham?* A black and white sheepdog padded into the yard through a red brick archway. *Here, Chip, to me, boy.* A heavy-set man followed in sturdy boots to leave a trail of mud and bits of straw across the cobbles. *Good morning, Mr. Downing.* The man looked straight through Theodore and walked on. *They can't see me. Why can they not see me?*

Theodore shuffled forward past the old hay barn and along a track edged on either side with a dozen well-stocked apple trees. His parents stood by the door of their cottage up ahead, hand-in-hand. Even through the blur, he could see they looked happy. Minnie ran up to hug them, and they hugged her back. *Father, I'm home. Mother, wait for me.* Theodore ran, eager to hold them, too, but his feet felt heavy, as if he wore shoes made from stone. He wanted to join them so much, to be back among his family and live on the farm once again.

A terrifying vision stopped him in his tracks. The sky turned black and a fiery smog billowed through the air. A roar rang out, long and loud. Theodore stumbled back as a huge, gnarled claw reached slowly over the thatched roof of the cottage, crushing their home with a single blow. *Rakista!* When the dust and the smoke cleared, only smashed bricks and blackened timber beams remained. The cottage was a ruin and his family had vanished. *Get away, Minnie. Run everybody. Run, run, run!*

***

He awoke cold and breathless, bathed in a sheen of sweat. *Just a dream,* he told himself. *I was just dreaming. It felt so real.* It took over an hour, but sleep returned, this time without the visions of the beast or the cottage they had once called home.

At first light, Theodore was ready to set out on the trail of his sister. Hints of his upsetting dream still teased his drowsy mind. As expected, the Queen would permit none of her soldiers to join him on this uncertain journey, however, she had granted that the boy be supplied with ample food-packs, a makeshift backpack to bear them, and the largest waterskin they could find.

Rhal had been busy, too. During the night, he had scoured the armoury to track down the 'giant' spear of the legendary warrior, Grolt, a Borini who had once stood a clear hand taller than any of his comrades. The weapon was finely crafted, feather light and as sharp as a razor blade. It felt barely a short spear in Theodore's hand. Still, such a vital weapon would at least bring him some protection and confidence. In this moment, he needed both equally. He needed all the help he could get.

Gifted tailors had done their best to fashion a hooded cloak to fit the boy's larger frame, using a turquoise silk drape acquired from a backstreet theatre. "The fabric appears rather delicate," Rhal explained. "But I can assure you, this garment will help keep the icy winds at bay and serve as a cool screen under a fierce sun."

Theodore was eager to begin. Eager, but terrified. He had little idea how he would actually save Minnie, even if he could find her, not to mention the dreadful creatures who held her captive. *I have to try. I have to.*

"Come on, Theo. You can do this." A radiant morning

sun warmed his body as he trekked away from the Borini city, up and over the foothills and north towards what the Borini called the Aradine Mountains. Their peaks lay hidden by fingers of wispy grey cloud, and in the sky directly overhead, a single white hawk floated the currents, a silent ghost among the clouds.

To climb up and over the mountains was never the plan. Instead, Theodore would seek a hidden tunnel carved through the mountains, the Aradine Path. Rhal had spoken to him before leaving Galenta, detailing a secret passageway partway up the slopes, and where the location of the entrance could be found.

"The Vorath are unaware of the shortcut," the Borini promised. "They shall be forced to take the west road, around the wide base of the mountain range, en route to their northern lands. By taking the Aradine Path, your chances of catching them up on the far side shall greatly increase."

That was the plan, at least. It was his only plan.

Theodore's confidence faded as the Aradine Mountains loomed larger with each exhausting step. He trudged past determined, wind-swept trees that clung to the ground, with their trunks bent low by the relentless gusts blowing down from higher up. It was almost midday by the time the ground took a noticeable upward slant, where a crisp, frosty scent carried on the wind and tremendous wedges of bare mountain rock pushed up through the soil and grass like craggy stone fists.

Even a tenth of the way up the mountainside, the view was spectacular. Theodore paused to catch his breath. He took a long drink from his waterskin and looked to the east, where the Aradine peaks curved inland, grey and dominant. In the opposite direction, the mountains ran straight, overlooking a rugged stretch of foothills that rolled and dipped. He could see glens and groves of dark green pine, hemlock, and spruce trees sheltered from the wind. Far beyond, a vast region of barren rock and endless dunes stretched all the way to the western horizon. And, of course, the ocean dominated to the south, wave upon wave glinting as far as his eyes could see.

"I'll get to you Minnie. I promise I will."

He struggled on into a bitter wind that chilled his hands and face, creeping around gnarled rock outcrops and across fields of damp, ankle-deep heather. Where great scree slopes scarred the mountainside, a good foothold was hard to find, slowing his progress further. Thick, tangled bushes grew wild across the lower slopes, too, sprouting between babbling streams crusted with thin ice that crunched under his feet.

The rim of a cavernous sinkhole seemed as good a place as any to rest. Theodore crouched beside the chasm, listening to an unseen torrent gush through the darkness below. "I'm close." *I must be.* According to Rhal's directions, the entrance to the mountain tunnel lay concealed further up among the barbs and thorns.

The temperature plummeted by mid-afternoon. A blanket of gloomy cloud drifted across the sun, threatening to bathe the landscape in rain. Thoughts turned to his sister as he searched among the undergrowth and rocks, polished smooth by the elements. *Stay strong, Min, I'll get to you.*

A sinister cackle startled him back to the present. Theodore jumped back in shock at the sight of a wicked-looking, impish creature clinging to the rocks close by. "Keep back," his voice squeaked. The creature was no larger than a crow, with claws at the tips of its black, leathery wings. A sharp, angry face, pitted with bitter red eyes, glared down at him.

Before Theodore could even think to run or call out again, the imp launched forward with a wild screech. It was on him quicker than the snap of a thumb and forefinger, sinking pin-sharp fangs into the flesh of his shoulder and slashing needle-like claws an inch from his face. He cried out and fell to his knees, overwhelmed by the vicious assault.

The attack ended as swiftly as it had begun, however, as the imp slumped to the ground, quivering, pierced by a single short arrow. A little way down the slope, a giant armoured stag beetle scuttled closer, flexing two powerful mandibles. A hooded Borini sat upright in the saddle strapped to its shell, looking left and then right, bow in hand, poised to see off any further threats.

A Borini soldier. But how? Whatever the reason, Theodore was more than delighted to see the stranger. He rushed over and kicked the scraggy corpse into a bush. "You came just in time. Thank you." The bite at his shoulder throbbed. "Who... who are you?"

The Borini gave no answer; instead, he ushered his mount at a canter up the slope. Theodore didn't hesitate to follow. They heard another cackle less than ten paces on, and then another, reverberating between the walls of a narrow gully up ahead. Three imps hovered in the wind, dark and menacing, with a further two crawling across a ledge to the left, hissing through barbed pink fangs, ready to pounce.

It was all too much. Theodore panicked and fled through the thickets, completely outnumbered, desperate to escape the growing mob of assassins.

"Up there... go, between the rocks," the stranger shouted after him.

More imps swooped in to join the ambush, screeching and hissing. "Get back," Theodore screamed. "Get away from me!" He stumbled to a knee but pushed himself back up to weave between the thistles and boulders, gripping the wooden handle of his spear tight to fend off his attackers.

He tripped again beside the trunk of a fallen tree and instantly felt the stab of tiny claws through the fabric of his cloak. "Get off me!" Theodore lashed out with his spear, catching an imp across the face with a fierce strike to leave it shrieking and writhing in agony. He moved again, and there, only a stone's throw ahead, he spied it: the dark entrance to the Aradine Path, partly hidden under a slanting ledge of pale rock and wilted vines. An age-old tree stood to the right of the cave, curved into the shape of a scorpion's tail, just as Rhal had described.

Move, Theo, move! he urged himself, but already it was too late. The imps came at him like a flock of ravenous gulls dive-bombing a shoal of sardines. Claws and fangs tore at his clothes and legs and arms, desperate to keep the boy out in the open. "Help! Get them off me!"

Aid came in the form of an arrow. A volley of arrows, in fact, loosed from inside the cave to repel the attack. *The Borini... how did he get in there so quickly?* Theodore staggered into the passageway, breathing hard.

One by one, the winged imps fell, each caught by a precisely aimed arrow. Soon, only a pile of spindly black bodies remained. The few imps to survive quickly gave up the chase, choosing instead to feast on an easier meal—their slaughtered brothers who lay twitching across the ground. Grim nibbling and the sound of snapping bones eventually faded, replaced by the incessant wind buffeting the landscape. The foul scent of black blood hung in the air a little while longer.

Theodore leant against the tunnel wall, rubbing his

shoulder. "Thank you. They would have torn me apart if not for you. What *were* those things?"

"Hydaks," answered the tiny figure, peering out from the tunnel. "It is highly unusual to find them so far down the mountains, especially in daylight. They usually hunt much further up the slopes."

"Hydaks? Awful creatures. I hope they don't like tunnels."

"We are safe in here... from Hydaks, at least." The stranger secured his bow and threw back the grey hood of his woollen cloak. He looked stockier and a touch shorter than Rhal, but his emerald eyes gleamed with a similar zest in a friendly round face. "I am Zilicarillion, Royal Guard to the Queen. She has sent me to assist on this quest, to ensure you find your sibling. This is a true honour, Master Reed."

His shoulder throbbed, and his head spun with confusion. "Assist me?" Theodore shuffled over the pebbled floor. "But the Queen, she said the Borini couldn't fight, Zilla... cari... Zilkal..."

"Please, call me Zilic."

Theodore covered his face as Zilic ignited a lantern to illuminate the cave. His eyes adjusted to see his saviour fully. The Borini warrior wore light studded leather under his cloak, with immaculate silver armour at his chest and shoulders, gilded with ornate swirls and markings. High leather boots hugged his narrow legs, and like his Queen, not a single hair grew upon his smooth, bronzed head.

"We cannot risk a conflict with the Vorath," Zilic explained. "Their numbers are too great. Our people are safe, and for now, of little concern to them. I am here in secret, sent by my Queen to guide you. I shall be your eyes, and I will protect you as best I can."

For a moment, Theodore fell silent, allowing the words to sink in. Guilt washed over him suddenly. *How could I have been so selfish?* He had only ever thought of himself and Minnie, not once about the Borini and their wellbeing. If they risked their lives by battling the Vorath to save his sister, it could have sparked a confrontation, even a full-scale war. *Think of others, you fool. Mother and Father taught you better than that.*

"Remain here," Zilic ordered. He slipped back out into the open to reclaim his spent arrows and stashed them neatly into a quiver upon his return. "This is Neup," Zilic spoke again, introducing his oversized beetle. "Neup is a Terap. They have long been companions to the Borini; loyal, brave, and fearsome in battle." The Terap clicked what may have been a greeting.

"He's magnificent." *A Terap. How incredible,* he thought. *I wish Minnie could see this.* "Fearsome is the word I would use, too." Theodore gazed at the Terap, a formidable sight so close up. Round eyes shone like jet-black orbs on either side of its stocky squared head, with fuzzy antennae quivering above. Curved mandibles and tough serrated jaws emphasised its daunting appearance. Its solid, domed shell could hardly have been glossier, reflecting a distorted, weary face back at him, a face he barely recognised.

Zilic took Theodore's backpack and waterskin, adding them to the supplies already dangling from the bulky saddle strapped to Neup's back. "You would travel more swiftly, unburdened. We should reach the Aradine Path before nightfall."

Theodore frowned and peered around the tunnel. "I thought *this* was the Aradine Path?"

"Not quite." Zilic leapt up into his saddle. "The true gateway to the Aradine Path lays a little further on." He whistled twice and steered Neup along the tunnel, deeper into the heart of the ancient mountains. The lamp light traveled with them to leave the secret entrance hidden in darkness once again.

Part 1 · Chapter 6

Walk a perilous path

Theodore trailed behind Zilic and his Terap for an hour or more, still shaken from his tussle with the Hydaks. He glanced back occasionally to make certain none of the frightful imps were sneaking up behind them. None were.

The tunnel steadily widened and emerged on to a broad ledge. Bone-grey roots sprouted down through the ceiling and from the walls on either side, and the deep chasm that lay beyond was so vast it could easily have swallowed an entire cathedral. Theodore looked up to see a bleak evening sky through a craggy opening high above, where heavy rain fell in to soak the walls and knotted trees growing from every crevice, clinging to the rocks, reaching up desperately for a glimmer of sunlight.

"Behold, the gateway to the Aradine Path." Zilic hopped down to stand beside Neup, raising his lantern to illuminate the imposing scene.

Theodore stared across a flat stone bridge that spanned the chasm, leading over to a towering granite archway in the shadows, flanked either side by colossal, smooth stone columns. "It's enormous!"

"It is as you say." The Borini set to work gathering wood for a fire, snapping brittle tree roots and arranging them into a neat pyramid.

"What are you doing? We can't stop now."

"You must rest." Zilic said calmly. He added a sprinkling of pine resin and used flint and steel to light the kindling. *Clink. Tap.*

"But… we need to get to Minnie."

"You are also injured, Master Reed."

Theodore brushed himself down. "It's just my shoulder, that's all. One of those little monsters bit me."

"You will be of scant use to anyone weary and wounded. Besides, this rain will surely slow the Vorath's progress through the night."

Theodore slumped down beside the fire, watching the rain dash against the bridge and drip from the branches growing around the ledge. *I should be with her,* he thought. *She must be terrified.*

Zilic moved away to retrieve a cloth pouch in Neup's saddlebag. "Please remove your cloak, Master Reed." He smeared a sour-smelling ointment over the teeth marks on the boy's skin and wrapped the wound in a soft cotton bandage.

"Thank you, Zilic," he said, impressed with his tidy dressing. "A fighter *and* a healer. You're full of surprises."

"You are most welcome," said Zilic. "The bite from a Hydak I can remedy, but try not to harm yourself further. I'm afraid my healing skills have limits."

Theodore stifled a yawn and settled against the tunnel wall. Hiking up the foothills for an entire day had left him thoroughly drained. He pulled his cloak tight and his eyes grew heavy. "Have you ever seen the Vorath?"

"Only from afar." Zilic knelt to stoke the fire as the twilight shadows deepened. "While the Vorath are said to roam more freely to the north, the Aradine Mountains have kept the Borini and our city all but hidden to them. They rarely venture so far south. My people are fortunate."

"Minnie wasn't fortunate." *I should have been there to protect her.*

"This is true," said Zilic. "I shall do everything in my power to have her returned to your side."

After a long silence, Theodore spoke again. "Do you have a family, Zilic?"

"An uncle," he nodded, then smiled. "Tasked, it seems, to provide eternal taunts and japes at my expense."

"Oh. He doesn't sound very nice."

"Quite the opposite. Olenious and I share a dear attachment. In truth, he is like a father to me, a faithful friend. And there's Neup, of course," Zilic added, giving the Terap's hard shell a pat. "We are a rather small family."

Theodore stared into the flames, listening to the wood snap and crackle. "Mine too." *I suppose Aunt Cordelia counts as family,* he considered, *though she never once made us feel like it.*

"We shall succeed, Master Reed. You have my word."

"Thank you, Zilic. I'm so glad you're here. I'm not sure I could do this alone. Minnie's all I have left... she's everything to me."

Zilic topped the fire and rummaged through his supplies. "You should eat. It will be a long trek through the mountains, one that shall require all of your strength, and..." Before his words were done, the boy had slumped into an uneasy sleep, snoring gently into his chest.

***

Breakfast was a cold, damp affair. Beads of moisture clung to Theodore's cloak and his fingers ached from a chill in the air, shivering as he held blocks of cheese and pear halves up to his mouth. The rain had thinned a little during the night, although the patch of morning sky visible through the opening high above remained a dreary shade of slate grey.

Zilic secured their supplies below Neup's saddle and led the way over the stone bridge, hopping over and around the puddles trickling over the edge. Theodore ignored the rain to keep his eyes fixed on the doorway ahead, marvelling at its sheer size, imagining the incredible effort it must have taken to build such a structure.

"Are you ready?" Zilic slipped his bow over a shoulder and unhooked a small lantern from his belt.

Theodore flinched as three speckled doves burst from a nook beside the entrance, wheeling around the chasm and up through the opening. "I'm ready." His shaky tone suggested otherwise.

Mica flecks in granite sparkled as they drew closer to the archway. "Stay close." Zilic said quietly. He gave the glass cap above the lantern a twist to increase the light.

They entered together, side by side, along a wide, sandy hallway. Tatty sheets of cobweb hung down from the dry stone walls, with oval passageways disappearing into darkness. The hall gradually narrowed to a pinch beyond a rubble heap where the ceiling had partially collapsed. From here, the hallway looked to be no more than a roughly cut tunnel, much like the passageway they had entered from the mountainside, damp and confined.

"How long will it take to make it through the mountain?" Theodore asked.

"A day, perhaps. Maybe longer."

Neup clicked in agreement.

"A day!" *Minnie could be miles away by then.*

"Patience and caution are needed, Master Reed."

"But my sister, she's…"

"She will not be abandoned."

I remember giving Minnie a similar promise, Theodore mused, chewing his lip.

"I am also keen to keep you and I from harm. For now, focus on the present. Countless pitfalls await us. Further on, the walls and passageways are able to shift and move as freely as you and I walk, leading the unsuspecting into a darkness they may never return from."

"This does seem like a strange place," Theodore agreed. His words echoed through the narrowing passage.

"Indeed; I never imagined I would return here."

"What? You've been here before? When was that?"

Zilic hopped up to his saddle before answering. "Some years ago now. Every Borini warrior with the ambition to serve and protect our people must navigate the Aradine Path, to prove their worth. The journey here is an invaluable experience."

The passage ran straight for some time before twisting one way and then another to avoid dark shafts of unknown depths, and through lofty chambers held up by sandstone pillars. Stalactites hung down from the shadows like giant, glistening teeth, with moisture dribbling down on to an equal number of stalagmites below.

Theodore listened with fascination along the way as Zilic spoke more about the trials and hardships he had overcome to be enlisted as a Royal Guard. "You must have nerves of steel," he said, astounded at the incredible bravery shown by the Borini. "I wouldn't dare to do even *half* of those things."

"Do not dismiss your own courage." Zilic pulled on Neup's reins to look down at the boy. "During my own training, I was never the strongest or the quickest. Even my skill with a bow could hardly be described as remarkable. But with tenacity and resilience, I rose to become a Royal Guard. Never give up, Master Reed. The fortitude you have already shown to make it this far is to be highly commended. You are far braver than you think."

A warm rosiness spread over Theodore's cheeks. "Thank you, Zilic. You're right, I can do this." *For you Minnie, I'll be as brave as any warrior,* he vowed.

The companions pressed on after a brief rest and a welcome drink of water. Occasionally, the tunnel opened out into enormous caverns where window slots and doorways vanished into the walls, carved from the rock so very long ago. All were unlit and empty. Only a few rotting timbers remained of the walkways and ladders and ramps leading inside.

"Who built this place?" asked Theodore. "It's so incredible. It must have taken a hundred years to build. A thousand!" His voice echoed.

"It is as you say," Zilic replied. "Whoever once lived here, they left a long time ago. Karadas has been a home to many civilisations; some remain, but most are now only myth."

"Maybe it was the Guardians? The Queen told me they were old."

"The Guardians of Zell-Ku, as they are better known, existed long ago," Zilic said, steering Neup around a crumbled water well. "But no, it was not them. The Guardians did not hide in the dark, in caves. It is said that they lived in great sea towers around the coast to watch over the land."

"The Warlocks, perhaps. Who were they?" asked Theodore, highly intrigued by the idea of magical creatures actually being real.

"The Guardians are no more; the Warlocks also," Zilic whispered. "Once we are safely through this section of the mountain, I shall tell you more. For now, we must be silent; now is not the time. Other forces still dwell here. We would do well to avoid them if we are to pass through the mountain unnoticed."

"Really? What kind of..." A frown and raised eyebrow from the Borini were enough to subdue the boy's wonderment. "Sorry."

Theodore felt his way along the tunnel, brushing his fingers against the damp, sandy walls, conscious now of every sound he made. Each breath and every step seemed to echo twice as loud as it had before. On and on they marched, hour after tiresome hour, over narrow brick bridges, up stone stairs and down stone steps, left, and then right, never straying from the path before them. Tufts of slimy moss, an ash white millipede, and the flutter of unseen bats were the only signs of life they encountered along the way.

Light from their lantern burst forward to caress the smooth walls of a wide circular chamber where the tunnel came to an end. A peculiar metallic aroma hung in the air and a gentle hum could be heard purring deep below their feet. Even through squinted eyes, Theodore could not make out a ceiling, nor an exit.

"Remain here," said Zilic, coaxing Neup out to the centre of the chamber.

Theodore gave a nod, watching the Borini hop down to inspect an uneven floor fashioned from a hundred ceramic tiles, each a different size and varied shade of grey. *What's he doing?* Not one tile lay level; most sank down, while others tilted upwards. "It's a dead end, Zilic. There must be a different path, something we missed?"

"You must learn patience, Master Reed," Zilic replied. He tapped each tile gingerly with a tiny bare hand.

Boom. Without any warning, a stone door at their back slammed down to seal the chamber. Theodore fell forward, terrified by the sound, crashing hard against the tiles with heavy knees and flailing hands. *You clumsy, ham-fisted oaf. Why is it always you, Theo?*

Zilic froze, fearful in anticipation.

A dull hiss echoed around the chamber, and an eerie silence followed.

Then, steadily, to their horror, the doom descended.

Part 1 · Chapter 7

Dark delirium

A handful came at first, falling like hail from the blackness above. Hundreds followed, and then a thousand more, countless yellow pebbles raining down into the chamber, rattling off the walls and floor, filling the air with a sulphurous dust that stung their eyes and choked their lungs.

Theodore raced over to the wall to avoid the worst of the avalanche. "What's going on?" he yelled through the clatter. *Pang, pang, ping.*

"A trap, it would seem." Zilic coughed and jabbed at each tile in turn. "One trigger to bury us alive, which you have worryingly discovered. And another to reveal an exit… which I hope to now find."

Dust rose in plumes as the barrage continued, dashing against the tiles and colliding into one another to quickly cover the floor. *Ping, ping, pang.* Neup and the Borini had almost vanished by the time a low rumble vibrated through the chamber.

"Zilic!" Theodore peered through his fingers to see a stone block slide out from the wall close by. Another followed, almost clouting him in the ear. "You did it… you did it!" Ten, twenty, then thirty steps emerged, unhurriedly, spiralling up into the darkness. The noise was deafening, stone grinding against stone.

"Go!" cried Zilic, surging over to the wall. "Climb up. Quickly. We have to move!" He beckoned Neup with a shrill whistle and darted up the stairs.

Theodore felt his way up blindly, struggling to breathe.

"Hurry!" Zilic streaked back down, pulling urgently at the boy's arm. "You must hurry."

Tears streamed from his eyes. "I can't see. Help me, Zilic!"

Then the panic truly set in. A jolt passed though the staircase, and every step eased deliberately back into the wall; yet another cruel trick.

"No! No! No!" He had to move now. Theodore blundered up and around the chamber wall, dabbing at his watery, dust-filled eyes.

The steps were vanishing fast, melting away one after the next. Theodore inched ever higher. Perspiration ran down his face as he dragged himself up and into a cramped, grainy shaft at the top, seconds before the last block vanished with a muffled thud. His shoulder ached and his eyes burned, but up ahead, a dim light offered hope. *A little further... and then... and then we'll be through.*

Theodore breathed a disappointed sigh as he slithered from the shaft. Instead of the exit from the mountain he had hoped for, they had merely arrived in yet another corridor. At the very least, this one was green and almost welcoming.

"You must take care, Master Reed," Zilic panted, helping the boy to his feet. "The tunnels here are filled with peril. There is danger everywhere."

"I'm sorry, the door fell, and..."

"Step only where I step. This place will be the end of us both if we do not work together."

The last of the day's light slanted in through a dozen bore holes high above, twinkling in a water duct running along the floor of a lengthy hall. Dark green ivy and golden orchids clung to the walls, filling the air with a pleasant, fresh scent, and tiny black bees buzzed from flower to flower, gathering nectar.

Theodore retrieved his waterskin and backpack and sat on a low ledge beside Zilic. The pair shared a sparse meal of pickled mushrooms and thin breads, washed down with a sweet lemon drink from a small oak keg clipped to Neup's saddle. With no kindling for a fire, they made do with the lantern to keep the growing darkness at bay.

"Rest a while," said Zilic, flicking a mushroom over to Neup. "The Aradine Path must not be rushed. Better that we make it through slowly, than not at all."

Theodore nodded. This time, he had no complaints. But after an hour or more, he remained restless, unable to settle fully. He quietly recounted the morning he awoke on the beach—Solar Beach, as Rhal had named it—all alone, and the unrelenting storm that had brought him to the shores of Karadas. His description of the great steel ship, the Titanic, seemed to impress Zilic greatly. "An entire city on the ocean," the Borini had commented.

Eventually, exhaustion and the light trickle of water lulled him to sleep.

***

How long Theodore had slept, he could not recall, but on being roused by his companion, he and Zilic continued their journey.

The hallway curved in a wide arc to the right, illuminated part way down by the morning sunlight shining in from above. Carved heads jutted from the ivy-clad walls on either side, with water seeping and burbling from narrow mouths and down to the duct running along the floor. They saw stone fish and stone snakes, eagles, horses, and the head of a boar, as well as other daunting faces that neither of them recognised.

"Amazing, aren't they?" said Theodore. He pointed up at the faded sketches, scrawled glyphs, and symbols mapped out across the ceiling. "Do you know what they all mean? It looks like a kind of story."

Zilic glanced up, shaking his head. "I am unfamiliar with their meaning. I did not notice them when I was last here. Some areas I remember; others, I do not."

At the end of the hallway, a circular doorway framed in cracked white stone led through to a vast cavern immersed in darkness. Its true size remained a mystery. A long, descending staircase disappeared down into a gloom so thick, Theodore feared it would swallow him up, to never see the outside world again. Still, he followed Zilic and Neup, regardless. He had little choice.

The granite steps seemed to go on forever, shiny in the lamplight. While the darkness remained constant, the temperature rose steadily, bringing a musty odour with it, and step by step the glow of a fiery oval pit down below grew wider and brighter with each passing minute.

"Tread carefully," Zilic warned. He led the way to a narrow walkway encircling the pit, leading to a second staircase opposite. "Keep close to the wall."

Steam wafted up in puffs as they shuffled forward, curling around their legs like ghostly fingers. The heat increased to an unbearable level. Sweat poured down Theodore's neck and face, and more than once, a dizziness almost overwhelmed him. It took every effort just to stay upright, gripping on to Neup's saddle to keep himself from keeling over. "Zilic, do you hear that?"

"Keep moving. It is an illusion. Nothing more."

The sound came from the pit: clearly the sound of a child's laughter. But more than that, soft laughter; a girl's laughter. "That sounds like Minnie!" Theodore could hear a boy, too, sobbing meekly. *Is that me? Why am I crying?*

"Block out the noise, Master Reed. This way, hurry."

Lightheaded and weak, Theodore caught up to Zilic at the foot of an identical staircase heading into the shadows, up and away from the simmering pit. Neup came hard at their heels with his clawed feet tapping lightly on the stone underfoot. "But it sounds just like me... and Minnie?"

"The mountains are full of mystery and cunning. You hear only what they want you to hear, to make you doubt yourself and bend those who come here against their will."

"It sounds so real." *Why is my voice so sad?*

Zilic shook his head and pulled at the boy's arm. "A sham, nothing more. Come, we must not linger here."

Theodore glanced back through the receding lamplight as they climbed up and away from the pit. The breath caught in his throat and his eyes grew wide at the sight of a dark, disturbing silhouette forming in the steam, wailing like a banshee. Another appeared, a shadowy girl clinging to the edge of the walkway, shrieking and laughing. The vision terrified him. He fled past Zilic, taking the steps two at a time in his haste to escape the cavern.

It took almost an hour to reach the top of the staircase. Instead of a white stone doorway, they found only a jagged split in the rocks. A short, cramped passage led through to a lofty chamber with walls moulded from glittering honeycombed stone.

"I am sorry you had to endure such an encounter," said Zilic. "It was an ordeal I had hoped to spare you from."

"That was awful." Theodore breathed in the sugary scent in the air and slumped to the floor, rubbing his aching legs. "What a horrid place." He finished the contents of his waterskin in one deep swig and wiped the dribbles from his chin with a sleeve. "If it means we can get to Minnie, this will all be worth it."

"Indeed. We are in agreement on that."

"So strange, though. It felt like she was right there beside me."

"Focus back on the present, Master Reed," said Zilic. He watched Neup pace around the chamber, pausing at various points to nibble at the rocks. "Once you reunite with your sibling, what do you plan to do then?"

Theodore shrugged and let out a long breath. "I honestly don't know. I hadn't thought that far ahead. Try to get home to England, I suppose." *Or somehow search for Aunt Cordelia*, he thought sullenly. "First, we'd need a boat."

"I regret that a boat would be of little use." Zilic leant against the wall to sharpen a silver dagger with an oilstone. The dagger was one of a pair the Borini kept sheathed at his belt. "It is said that the waters around Karadas are impassable."

Theodore forced a smile. "You sound like Rhal." He cupped his chin in his hands and sighed. "There must be a way to leave here?"

"None that I am aware of." Zilic brushed a thumb over the blade. "On our return to Galenta, I shall certainly help you search for a way to travel beyond our realm, to see you both home."

"You would do that... for me... and for Minnie?"

"It would be a privilege, Master Reed. Though I cannot promise we shall find a solution."

A warm smile spread over the boy's face, touched by the kindness shown by his tiny new friend.

They rested for only a short time. Theodore slipped his waterskin and backpack over a shoulder, ready to discover what other daunting schemes the mountains had to offer. Half a dozen honeycombed chambers lay ahead until the walls gradually narrowed and smoothed, leading into a dusty passageway tiled in black and crimson squares. The corridor turned right, and then left, and then right again, marked along the way with waxy grey streaks running down the walls from candle alcoves.

A heavy iron door stood ajar where the passageway

came to an abrupt halt up ahead, thick with rust and steeped in shadow. Flowers and vines carved into a stout timber frame had a diseased, frail look about them. Every inch appeared splintered and tainted by woodworm.

"Wait here," said Zilic. Grit crunched under his boots as he moved to investigate. Chalky water seeped under the door, snaking across the floor and down to an unseen crevice with a restful murmur.

"Is there a way through?"

The Borini gave no answer. He crept forward with his bow raised, peering through the doorway with wide emerald eyes. "Curious," he muttered.

"Maybe we should go..."

"Here, Master Reed." Zilic placed the lantern into the boy's hand and went to rummage through his supplies for a rope. With Neup's great pulling power, they heaved the door open a little more. Its ancient hinges groaned as if in agony.

"What do you see?" Theodore asked, unsure he actually wanted to know.

"Remain with Neup." Zilic stepped through the doorway with a second, smaller lamp, tiptoeing around the water, not allowing any to touch his dusty black boots. The lantern burned even brighter as he twisted the glass cap, bathing the chamber in beaming white light.

Theodore peaked inside to see water leaking from a crack high in the wall, pooling around twenty, perhaps thirty, stone blocks, laid out throughout the chamber. The water covered every inch of the floor. Nine crumbling brick doorways stood along the far wall, each marked with a unique symbol above. Fire, a tree, a sword, and a crescent moon were the only symbols he could make any sense of. The others had either faded or were simply a mystery to his eyes.

"A burial chamber," Zilic whispered, pointing to the stone blocks. "Resting place to the fallen warriors of age-old battles." Tombs not only lined the floor but also the hollow ledges that rose high into the shadows above.

Zilic hopped on to a nearby casket with the grace of a wildcat, studying the water. An anxious look swept over his face as a ripple caught his eye. "Climb up, Master Reed. Come away from the water."

Theodore used his spear as a prop and clambered on to a tomb. He lifted his lantern higher and peered around the room, listening to the trickling water. "What is it? What do you see?"

"Just the light playing tricks," Zilic reassured him. "Follow me."

Neup took a different route. The Terap climbed up the wall using six hooked feet to grip on to the sandy rock with ease. Theodore made his way across the caskets, further into the burial room.

Zilic froze as the lid of the fifth tomb tilted and knocked loudly under the boy's feet, stone striking stone to send a procession of ripples dancing across the surface. "Careful. We must not disturb the water."

"Sorry." Theodore pressed on, this time with added care. The sense of concern in his tiny companion was more than apparent.

It felt like an eternity before Zilic arrived at the back wall to stand beside one of the brick doorways. "This is our path," he whispered, pointing to the lintel above, marked with a dull crimson triangle.

No warning came.

In the blink of an eye, the water exploded beneath Neup. Thick translucent tentacles reached up from the water to clamp around the stranded Terap, dragging him down to the surface.

"Neup!" Zilic cried out. He and Theodore looked on in horror as the frightening reality of their situation became clear. It was no creature they needed to fear; the water itself was the genuine threat. Below their feet lay a terrifying living entity in liquid form, waiting patiently to snare its prey and drag them to their doom.

Zilic surged over to the Terap faster than Theodore believed possible, vaulting from one tomb to the next at an astonishing pace with his cloak streaming behind him. "To the door," he yelled. "Get out of here. Go. Run!"

Theodore's stomach churned, and fear almost stopped his heart. He held his breath and hurdled the final caskets as fast as he dared, fearful that the water would coil around his legs at any moment. A final, exhausted leap delivered him to the far wall. He scrambled back and forth, desperately searching for the doorway displaying the crimson triangle. *Crack.* His lantern smashed against the brick and steadily faded to black, leaving every doorway in darkness.

"Run!" Zilic screamed again. His daggers slashed uselessly at the water strands and his lantern swayed at his belt to make every shadow lurch and pitch.

He could barely watch. Theodore's eyes welled with tears. "Zilic!"

"Get away from here. You have to run!"

"I won't leave you." *He needs me,* Theodore urged himself, watching the tentacles gather around his friend, ready to strike. *But what can I do?* Before he could muster his inner courage, the Borini cried out and vanished under a swirling mass. *This can't be happening... this isn't right. How can this be happening?*

The water settled and a small lantern bobbed on the surface, flickering, the only evidence that Zilic and Neup had even been here at all.

Part 1 • Chapter 8

Whisper on the Water

"I hate this wretched place." Theodore collapsed at the top of a hundred widening steps with his heart straining with sorrow. *I wish we'd never come here.* His spear clanked loudly as he hurled it across the cold stone floor of a towering hallway up ahead. Fresh air wafted in from the outside world between a row of angled pillars at the far end of the hall, where blazing sunlight streamed in to make the exit appear like the opening to a giant's forge.

The striking sunset went unnoticed. Theodore fastened the lantern to his backpack and trudged mournfully from the mountain tunnel, unsure if he had even gone through the correct door. He had no way to know for sure now.

He alone had survived the Aradine Path. Theodore crouched on a worn step below a tall granite archway, rubbing his forehead in dismay, contemplating his seemingly ill-fated existence. *Gone,* he thought sadly. *All of them. Mother. Father. My sister... and now Zilic. It must be me... I must be cursed!*

A weary huff escaped from his lips. He looked down the mountainside and out over an enormous shimmering blue lake, stretching away from the base of the mountains. "How do I save Minnie now?" he muttered to himself. "I have to try; I have to."

Even in the amber glare of the sun, his eyes could just about make out the road beyond the lake's north-western shore; a fine grey line weaving across the landscape. Rhal had been certain the Vorath would travel along the road en route to their lands in the north. It looked to be a gruelling, lengthy walk around the lake to the left, and even further if he chose the opposite shore. Not to mention the fact that he still had the mountain to descend. *I have to go one way or the other. But which?*

"Down first," he muttered. Tilted stone blocks dragged down by time led away from the archway and around a sheer drop, all the way to a rough gravel path coated in moss and loose rubble, zig-zagging down the mountainside. At steeper sections, he could see steps cut into the rock.

Theodore let out an uncertain sigh and began his trek down to the lake, using his boots and spear to brush aside the grasping brambles and burly thistles poking up from the ground. "Ouch!" He quickly learned to avoid the stab of their blood red spines.

An erratic wind blew east to west across the mountainside; elements above and below combining to heighten Theodore's misery. Soon, his legs ached from what felt like ten thousand steps. A dry mouth and belly rumble were a reminder it had been many hours since his last decent meal. But with Neup and Zilic now gone, his appetite had faded. No amount of food or water would remedy their loss.

The sun sank steadily towards the western horizon, ready exchange places with the moon and the stars. It would not be long now. At that moment, as the wind dropped a touch, Theodore heard a sound; a muffled, almost imperceptible sound, one he couldn't quite place. "What *is* that?" he said to himself. "Please don't let it be a Hydak."

His eyes scanned the mountainside to his left and the dry, spindly undergrowth to the right. Quite how he hadn't seen it sooner, Theodore could not have said; the bird hardly blended in with the landscape.

A small white hawk perched on an outstretched branch no more than twenty feet back, peered down at him with glossy black eyes. He recalled seeing similar birds afloat on the warm winds above Galenta. Much like a Terap, the white hawks shared a loyal, almost symbiotic relationship with the Borini people.

"Hey little bird." *Perhaps he's here looking for Zilic?* he wondered. Theodore took a strip of smoked fish from his pack and flicked it on to a mossy verge close by. In seconds, the hawk obliged, eager to claim the prize on offer. "Hello, you pretty thing." He watched the fish disappear in a single gulp. "You're from Galenta, aren't you? The Borini city." *You must have flown for miles.* "I hope you're here to help me."

The hawk made no reply. It simply stood and stared, with its head leaning to one side, hungry for further treats. A second fish strip barely touched the ground before the bird snaffled it up.

"I have to get over there," Theodore said, pointing at the far side of the lake. He could barely see the road now through the dusky twilight. "My sister needs me. I don't suppose you've seen her, have you?"

As expected, the bird gave no answer. Round, curious eyes looked back.

Theodore stumbled back on to the steps when the hawk suddenly flew at him, screeching and swooping down to peck at his arm. "That's all I have," he cried. "There's no more fish. Get away! What's got into you?" His mouth fell open as the bird whipped Minnie's rainbow bracelet from his wrist with a talon and hovered overhead. "You know where she is... you're trying to give me a sign, aren't you?"

The hawk circled twice and dropped the bracelet into the boy's lap before drifting left to right down the mountainside toward the lake. The water shone like liquid gold in the last light of the day.

Don't go. Theodore gathered up his pack and scampered down the path as fast as his legs would carry him, with his cloak and empty waterskin flapping behind him. "Hold on, wait for me. Come back!" A startled goat munching a grass verge leapt away from the path as he rushed by.

Dusk loomed by the time he reached the foot of the mountain. "Where are you?" he called out. *Where did you go, little bird?* He could see no sign of the hawk, nor a route around the lake to the left or to the right as he had hoped for. Instead, a cobbled path twisted around mounds of bare earth and half-dead trees towards a small lakeside hamlet.

As he drew closer, Theodore found it hard to imagine that anyone had lived in this desperate place for many, many years. *I don't like this,* he told himself nervously. *Not one bit.* Tall dry grass, blushed poppies, and nut-brown shrubs grew wild all around, but little else. Abandoned wooden huts stood in decay among an even greater number of charred ruins, every one casting an eerie shadow.

Rot and a bitter stink of stagnant water lingered in the air. The wind dwindled to a light breeze as Theodore entered the settlement. He looked around to see tangled nets draped over timber frames, and laying here and there in untidy heaps. "A fishing village," he guessed. *Fishermen must surely use a boat? There must be one here.*

Theodore broke into a jog and headed towards the shore, eager to find a boat to carry him across the lake. It didn't take long until he felt highly uneasy, sensing hidden eyes that never slept boring into his back. *What a miserable place,* he thought, peering around. A queer silence suffocated the gloomy scene, with only an occasional whistle of wind or creak of wood to break the hush.

"Little bird… are you here?"

The sun kissed the north-west lake shore to melt away in an orange haze. The sky turned pink and then dark grey, leaving Theodore all alone in the darkness. He quickened the pace again and arrived at the lakeside. The remains of a curving pier stretched out over the water, with its timber uprights jutting up into the night sky like a witch's gnarled fingers, worn and crooked.

"Boats!" He darted around a mound of tatty fishing nets, heading to where three boats lay on a shingle beach. Not one of them looked fit for his use.

Theodore flinched and froze. Tiny pimples rose on the skin of both arms. "Who's there?" The breath caught in his throat. Slowly, so slowly it was barely noticeable, a tall shadowy figure drifted behind an open, empty doorway back along the shore.

The sight filled him with a sudden panic. Theodore fumbled at his lantern, twisting the glass cap round and around. He dropped it to the ground when it refused to offer even a glimmer and turned his attention instead to the boat nearest to him: a narrow kayak with room enough for three. Even to a light touch, the slats crumbled to dust, the wood utterly rotten. Its sailing days were over. It would barely make decent firewood now.

A sour odour came on the breeze to turn his blood cold; a rancid stench of decay. The figure emerged again through the darkness, less subtly than before. A second appeared, and then a third, all dressed in long black shawls that dragged along the floor and hung down below where Theodore guessed their hands to be. He could not dare to think of what those hands might look like. They crept out from behind the bushes and blackened buildings, uttering sinister whispers.

"Stay back," he called out in a shaky voice, frantically checking the next boat, but that would not save him either. The hull had decayed even more severely than the first boat.

An upturned coracle was all that remained to him now. It looked almost like a giant turtle resting on the shingle, built from wicker and stretched hide. Theodore quickly flipped it over and dragged it out into the water. The chill of the lake gave rise to a shudder. "Please float," he begged. "Please, please float."

The coracle was weather-beaten and unsightly. However, to his great relief, it appeared to be intact and bobbed encouragingly on the surface. Theodore towed the coracle further and further out, pushing against the lakebed with his spear, desperate to be away from the horrifying wraiths.

Rusted fishhooks dangling from a frayed rope clinked and jangled with each thrust of his arms as he thrashed at the water. *Keep going... just a little further.* His limbs ached and the wicker hull dug deep into his chest. Every second was agony.

"Keep going," he screamed to himself, but his energy soon waned. His arms became limp, too drained to row any more. Theodore twisted around to see six slender figures stood at the water's edge like statues of the night, watching the coracle drift away. Even out on the water, under a star-studded sky, he could still smell their foul scent and hear their venomous whispers. Both chilled him equally.

"Danger everywhere," he muttered. *Zilic was right.*

Fireflies bounced across the surface of the lake, their tails aglow with vivid pinks and cool blues as Theodore paddled at a slow pace for an hour or more, leaving the eerie lakefront far behind, lost in the darkness. The exhaustion became too much all of a sudden, and he had to rest. His hands felt almost frozen, and his chest and arms throbbed. He pulled his cloak tight to fend off a chill in the air, allowing the coracle to float freely. For a while, he allowed his eyelids to close.

His eyes shot open at the sound of a whisper. *Did I sleep?* Theodore peeked through a chink in his hood to see a green light flickering in the distance, a peculiar vivid flame dancing upon the lake. "I must have slept," he whispered. "What is that?" The coracle jerked forward sharply, pulled by an unseen force, nudging Theodore back against the hull. "What's going on?"

A second flame popped and fizzed into life as the craft drew closer. More and more followed, encircling the coracle in a wide ring of sea-green fire. Theodore almost fell overboard as a slanting wedge of oily rock rose silently from the water, lifting the coracle from the lake and into the air. The tiny isle glistened in the eldritch green light, coated in clam shells and strands of black, oily weed. Dozens of silver-scaled fish flailed and flapped on the rock, desperate to return to the safety of the lake.

This must be a dream... it must be. Theodore stepped out from the coracle against his will, as if unconnected to his own body. An unusual desire urged him to clamber further up the rock and towards a slim hollow cut into the floor where a sombre blue light pulsed.

"Master Theodore," a deep, reassuring voice spoke. "Theodore Reed. I welcome you."

Theodore spun around. Dread swelled within his chest, fearful that the wraiths had somehow followed. "Who's there?" He was alone, all alone. "How do you know my name? Who are you?"

"I know of much, young one. In a time gone by, there were many who knew of me," came a cryptic reply. "Do not be fearful. You will come to no harm here." The voice spoke again after a momentary pause, allowing each word to resonate. "Your journey has led you to this place. To serve Karadas."

What on earth is going on? "I, I don't understand." *To serve Karadas?* "I can't... I just want my sister back. We don't belong here."

"My order are all but extinct," said the voice. "I appear here to you now in spirit only; the last Guardian of the Zell-Ku."

"The Guardians of Zell-Ku?" *They're real... the story was true?* What seemed so long ago now, in the comfort of her royal chamber, the Borini Queen and Rhal had spoken of the Guardians of old, the protectors of the veiled realm.

"The time has come, Theodore Reed. Accept this offering and restore peace to Karadas."

The light inside the hollow grew to an intense blaze, yet Theodore could not draw his eyes away. "Me? I... I can't, I don't know what..."

"The hour grows late, young one," the Guardian interrupted. "Seek the sea tower bordering the Jurkoon Desert. Look for me there. Accept this offering. Be swift. Be strong. Become the difference."

Before Theodore could summon a reply, an object appeared gradually in the hollow, suspended on invisible strands.

"What tower?" *What does all this mean?* His mind whirled in puzzlement. "I just… I can't. I need to find Minnie."

"Reach out and become the difference," the Guardian spoke one last time, his voice echoing to silence.

The desire became overwhelming. Theodore extended a shaky hand inside the hollow. The light vanished with a loud crack as his fingers closed around the object, followed by rumbling thunder, rolling away over the water.

"Where… where am I?" He snapped from his daze, icy cold and breathing hard, clawing his way back down to the coracle. The isle receded gradually back into the lake and a ghostly fog drifted forward to extinguish the circle of green fire.

Theodore settled in the coracle, exhausted, cold, and confused; all alone under the silvery glow of a hazy half moon. "What is this thing?" he whispered, unwrapping a square of white cloth from the object to reveal a magnificent curving dagger with a frosted crystal blade. A short ivory handle trembled in his hand below a solid bronze cross-guard. From hilt to tip, the dagger was a foot in length. Even in the sparse light of the moon and stars, it sparkled with untold energy.

It was all too much. The horizon lurched sickeningly, and Theodore's eyes rolled back. His head filled with a stifling haze and he collapsed into the basin of the coracle like a sack of straw before his world turned black.

Part 1 • Chapter 9

An endeavour of hope

For the second time in a matter of days, Theodore awoke in sodden clothes. On this occasion, he found himself slumped in a shabby, ruined coracle, snagged on the rocks a few feet from the lake's northern shore. A murder of crows watched on with beady red eyes, huddled in the rotting corpse of a leafless tree close by. Not one of them moved so much as a feather. Each one remained as still as a painted clay ornament.

Theodore's head buzzed, as if it was stuffed with wet wool. *It was a dream. It must have been,* he reflected. *But the dagger, the voice... I don't understand any of this.* He scooped his pack from the water and held up the dagger.

Its frosted blade flickered mysteriously in the light of the early morning sun. "What is this thing?" he mumbled. "It's beautiful."

For now, answers about the dagger, the Guardian, and where in the world Karadas actually lay would all have to wait. For now, all of his focus had to be on his sister. *Be safe, Minnie. I'll get to you soon.* Conscious of the watching red eyes, Theodore tucked the weapon inside his backpack, squeezed the water from his cloak and headed west along the lakeshore. The land to the north and further to the east appeared featureless and unforgiving; miles of barren marshland with a grassy hump here and there, but little else.

Grey cloud drifted overhead as Theodore topped up his waterskin and pulled his cloak tight. Rain felt imminent. He turned away from the lake with his plimsoles squelched on the boggy terrain underfoot, weary and cold, heading overland to where he hoped to find the road.

It was midday when he arrived at a cracked clay ridge studded with yellow and orange flowers. The road lay over the top, though in truth, it looked little more than a dry, muddy track close up. Leafy weeds and ferns moved in the breeze like limp green hands on either side, waving to any travellers. Clearly, no one had come this way in several days. There were no footprints or cart tracks to be seen, only spirals of dust twirling in pirouettes.

"The Vorath haven't passed by yet," he whispered to himself. "I'm sure of it." Theodore's spirit soared at the notion. *I can do this.* He clenched his fists. *I'll battle a hundred Vorath—a thousand—for my sister.* It felt as though there was still a chance to save Minnie.

Time, however, was not on his side; the enemy could arrive at any moment. Theodore needed a plan. To go in quick-tempered and impulsive would end in defeat and probably cost him and Minnie their lives. One thing was for certain: with Zilic and Neup no longer by his side, the Vorath would easily outnumber him. "Come on, Theo," he said into his hands. "Think, think, think." *What would Zilic do? What would Father have done?*

To the south, he could see the road snaking down the western slopes of the Aradine Mountains and on through a wide, flat valley, heading his way. "That's where they'll come from," Theodore decided.

Fields lay in the opposite direction; cramped fields running alongside the road stocked with oilseed and flaxen crop and freshly ploughed soil, filling the air with rich, syrupy aromas. Hedgerow and timber fencing separated each field, with a small farmstead nestled in the shadow of a maple tree grove less than half a mile away. He could see another farm in the distance, far away from the road. This one looked a little larger, with hay heaps, stables, and outbuildings, and a round stone house topped with well-worn thatch. Pale smoke rose lazily from two brick chimneys.

"Father would have used the farmland to hide." *I know he would.* Theodore tramped along the road, heading for the fields, before a sudden thought occurred to him. If the Vorath were to capture him, they would seize his strange new dagger and take him as a slave, just another hopeless slave. Cautious of that outcome, he took a swig from his waterskin and stashed it with his backpack and the dagger among the scrub. Only then did he dart across the road.

A herd of stocky mammals in the nearest field took little interest as he approached. Each animal looked to be a ton of raw sinew, with matted green hair reaching down to the ground. They ambled around on four stumpy legs with their heads hung low, ignoring the boy to focus instead on the grassy feast under their hooves.

Still, he kept a safe distance and his spear tilted. Theodore crept into their enclosure, squeezing through a bramble hedge and under a crooked, brittle fence. He couched low with his nose pinched to block out a powerful stench of dung, watching the road to the south. With the element of surprise on his side, he hoped—with luck—to cause a distraction, to snatch his sister, and to make a swift escape. Somehow.

"This is madness," he said aloud, shaking his head. "I'm no warrior." He chewed his lip and nibbled his fingernails. *What use will I be against the Vorath?* Worry turned over in his mind. *They'll tear me apart!*

He quickly became a bundle of nerves, racked with doubt as the enormity of the task dawned on him. Up to this point, he had yet to even lay eyes on the Vorath. He could only imagine them to be strong, well-armed, and certain to be skilled in combat. Even if only a handful arrived, it would be warriors against a boy of only thirteen; a complete mismatch. *I have no choice; I have to try.*

Theodore sat in wait behind a curtain of damp grass for over an hour. His legs were numb and gnats tormented him constantly, but he kept his eyes glued to the road. The drizzle came and went and then came again, then suddenly, when he had almost given up all hope, he heard a faint sound, maybe just a trick of the wind. "Please be you, Minnie." Soon, though, there was no denying it. The noise came clearly through the air: the sound of heavy hooves and boots stomping in unison.

The Vorath had arrived.

In his eagerness to see the enemy he would face, Theodore leant heavily on the fence and instantly regretted his decision to do so. The wooden slats gave way under his weight and clattered on to the road, taking him along with them.

Panic came first, but then a sudden spark took root in his mind; a sly notion, a daring idea that could make the enemy's numbers count for nothing. It was a bold plan. *This could actually work,* he thought.

"Come on Theo, work fast." He used his knees and the flats of both hands to smash more slats off their rusting nails, stashing the broken timber in the undergrowth. *This had better work.* He took a knee at the back of the field, away from the road, watching and waiting. *How can this work?* "This is madness!"

Hooves clomped, coming ever closer down the road. Leather creaked and shields and armour clinked. Spear tips and silver chrome helmets that shone like mirrors appeared over the hedgerow, followed by the roof of a wooden box cart, drawn by two large black horses.

It had to be now; hesitate and his chance would pass. "Come on," Theodore growled through gritted teeth. "Do it for Minnie." He charged forward with his spear pointed at the livestock close by. "Yah! Yah! Move!" he cried. The closest beasts reared and backed away, but he didn't stop there. Theodore waved his spear maniacally, poking and prodding at their thick green hides. "Yah! Yah!" As one, utterly dismayed, the animals rushed towards the road in a mass panic. The remaining herd followed, funnelling through the gap in the fence in a cloud of grass and flies and dust.

Spears and shields tensed as the enemy sensed the commotion. But it was already far too late. Their time to react had passed. A wall of horn, hair, and brawn burst from the field, smashing against the cart and surging over the dumbfounded soldiers whose screams and shrieks snapped to silence under the stampeding hooves. The herd scattered, bellowing and plodding away down the road and across to the scrubland beyond.

Theodore charged out behind them, ready to battle for his sister's life. When his eyes settled on the carnage laying all around, he knew there would be no battle today. Eight wiry figures lay across the track, trampled into the dirt, with their ink blue leather and chain mail garb torn and tattered. Metallic helms shaped like eggs kept their faces all but hidden. All he could see were the cracked leathery lips of their narrow mouths, filled with barbed teeth and festering sores. Not one of the Vorath moved. Incredibly, his plan had worked perfectly; the livestock had wiped out the entire troop.

"Where have you been?" Theodore called out as the white hawk returned to hover above the cart. "Off catching mice were you, while I..." And then he spied her. There she crouched inside the cart. His sister, his only sister, with her heart-shaped face the colour of milk. "Minnie!"

Theodore heaved open the splintered door to get to her. Even here she looked dainty. Minnie still wore her tatty black headband trimmed with feathers that matched her hazel eyes; she was a young double of their mother in every way, especially her plaited red hair that fell down over a shoulder. Her walnut-on-white checked dress had seen better days—matted with sand and torn at both the sleeve and hem. The black button boots on her feet had fared better, but not by much; both were scuffed and crusted with dried mud.

"Theo! Theo, you're here," she cried. Dimples formed in her smooth pink cheeks, and her eyes exposed the relief at seeing her brother.

He inched inside the cart and took Minnie gently by the hand. "Try not to move. Are you hurt?"

"I don't think so."

A smile grew to a grin as Theodore held out her rainbow bracelet. She wept with joy as he slipped it over her hand. "I prayed every hour I'd see you again."

"I knew I'd find you; I would never have left you, Minnie Mable." He would often call her by her middle name, Mable, in jest or frustration. Here and now, though, it was uttered purely from the heart.

The siblings clambered out of the cart and hugged warmly. Smashed timber, shields, spears, and grim bodies lay all around them. "Who are they?" asked Minnie with a shiver. "I woke up… and it was dark. I could hear the waves. Then they were there. They, they…"

"They're gone now," Theodore reassured her. "You're safe. Did they hurt you?"

"No, no… I'm not hurt, just scared. They surrounded me and locked me in that stupid cart. They *terrified* me, Theo."

"Shush now," he whispered, brushing the dust and

splinters from her shoulders. "They're called the Vorath. Not a friendly bunch, from what I've been told. I can't explain everything right now; we just need to go. It's so good to see you though, sis," he finished with a smile.

"Eden!" Minnie called out when she noticed the white hawk perched on a shattered wheel spindle. "Eden. You beautiful thing."

"Eden? You named him *Eden?* That little bird helped me to find you."

"I named *her* Eden," Minnie said, rushing over to stroke the bird's soft head. "She's a lady, not a gent. Eden came to me whenever it got dark. She brought me berries to eat, and even a shrew once, though I was never hungry enough for that!"

"'Ere, you. Be off," a stern voice called out. "What you pair been doin' to my herd?"

The siblings turned to see a short, dumpy-looking man marching along the road dressed in a well-worn canvas tunic and a wide-brimmed straw hat. He shuffled forward in battered brown boots to stand before the chaos strewn over the track. He was as wide as he was tall, with a freckled, sweaty face framed in a close-cropped beard. Russet eyes glared at the children above a pug nose flecked with tiny red veins.

Although Theodore and his sister stood a half-a-foot taller than the stranger—both were tall for their age—they had always respected their elders. They waited nervously, fearful of a scolding as the farmer crouched beside the fallen Vorath.

"I'm sorry, sir," Theodore said, tidying his hair to appear more presentable. "I didn't mean for all this. They took my sister. I had to free her. We'll pay for the damage, somehow. I could fix the fence... or help you round up the animals?"

A smile spread over the farmer's face as he rose. He clutched his bulging belly and chuckled, almost doubled over. "Bless you, young master. You done a splendid thing 'ere today. Horrid, cowardly beasts, them Vorath lot are. You've rid us of a few of 'em, at least... they take all they want, forcing us farmers year on year to feed their foul, stinkin' mouths."

"We didn't want to harm them," Minnie muttered, moving forward to join her brother.

"You be a big lad and lady. Where you be from?"

"We're not really from here, from this place," said Minnie. "I think we're a long way from home, far away from England."

He looked them up and down, scratching at his neck. "Hmm; don't think I ever 'erd of a town called England."

"I came from the far side of the mountains," Theodore added, pointing back towards the Aradine peaks.

"Borini be livin' over there. Did they put you up to this?"

Theodore felt unsettled and his eyes narrowed. *How does he know about the Borini? Who else knows they live there?* He certainly didn't want anyone to think this was their doing.

"Don't you be worryin', young sir," the farmer chuckled again, sensing the boy's reluctance to speak. "Them Borini folk be a grand bunch. They'll always be friends to the Narook. Milport won't be tellin' nobody about them."

"Narook?"

"Narook folk. Like me. We be 'avin' many an old friend in Karadas. Well, we did 'ave once. Till these *divils* started their trouble," Milport grumbled, kicking at a Vorath soldier with a boot. "You young'uns best be off. Take one of them there 'orses. Leave old Milport to tidy up this clutter."

"Thank you, sir," said Theodore. He hurried away to retrieve his backpack from the undergrowth. On his return, with help from his sister, they unhooked the smaller of the two horses, eager to be far away. Both he and Minnie had learned to ride from an early age back on the farm in Corsham, although neither had ever handled an animal as large as the one they now sat upon.

"Thank you again, Milport," Theodore called out, wheeling the horse around in a tight circle. "You're very kind; we won't forget this. Thank you, Milport. Farewell."

"You be takin' care now," Milport bowed. "Be safe."

The horse galloped along the road with the boy's heels pressed deeply into its flanks, around the great lake and toward the Aradine Mountains.

Theodore felt in total shock, amazed that his absurd plan had actually worked. There was only one place he could think of where he and his sister may find safety: Galenta, the Borini city. The Queen and her people might be the only hope left to them.

***

Raindrops fell to dot the road as the dust settled. Black silhouettes circled in the sky above, vanishing on the next breeze. A single feather spiralled to the ground at Milport's back as he worked to clear the road and fix the fence.

Little did he know that the keen red eyes of a dozen ravens and two dozen crows—loyal spies for the enemy—had witnessed everything. Once news of this treachery reached their master, the retribution would be swift, and it would be terrible.

Part 1 • Chapter 10

Mountain misery

Eden's wings were a blur in the wind as she struggled to keep pace with the horse. They raced along the rutted road, past the western shore of the lake and beyond, on and on, into a wide green valley where the Aradine Mountains parted.

Theodore tugged on the reins, easing their mount to a gentle trot under the cover of a sparsely lit pine grove. Birds tweeted in the treetops and a shallow stream gurgled through the undergrowth. A rabbit hopped across the road up ahead.

Minnie hardly noticed the peaceful setting. "Why are we slowing?" she asked. Eden caught up to land on the pack slung over her shoulder.

"There's still a long way to go." Theodore brushed the dust and sweat from his brow. "We need to give her a rest."

"Good girl. There now," Minnie whispered. She stroked the horse's sweat-soaked flanks, hoping her words would spur the animal back to a gallop immediately.

The road rose steeply by midday, snaking up the mountainside between blocks of weathered rock and around dusty scree slopes. Along the way, the children recounted very different tales of the previous few days. Each had a string of questions for the other, though neither had many answers.

Theodore recalled the morning he awoke alone on Solar Beach. He spoke of the horrifying beast, Rakista, and his encounter with the spider swarm with eyes as white as stars. He told his sister all about Galenta—the incredible Borini city—and his traumatic journey through the mountain tunnel. Both felt a deep sadness for Zilic and Neup. Minnie gasped at each part of the extraordinary tale, her young heart fluttering with each new revelation.

The relief at being reunited brought a genuine feeling of warmth and joy, despite all the horror the two had faced. Together again, but not nearly safe.

"Where is this place, Theo? How did we even get here?"

"I'm not sure. The lifeboat must have drifted a long way. Rhal—he's the Queen's aide—well, Rhal said that magic makes this entire land invisible."

"*Magic?* Like a magic spell?"

"I know. It sounds batty, doesn't it? They call this place Karadas; an island hidden from the rest of the world."

"That sounds like a nanny's tale; it can't be true." Minnie took a sip from their waterskin. "I just want to go home. I *hate* it here."

They cantered in silence for a while. Eventually, her brother spoke his mind. "We don't have a home anymore, Minnie. You know that. We're moving to America, remember... to live with Aunt Cordelia. If we ever get there, that is. Things won't be like they were before."

"Can't we just go back to Corsham, to the Downing's farm? I don't want to live with her." Minnie pulled a face. "Cordelia *hates* me. She only said she'd take us to please Grandfather. You know that's true, Theo."

"You shouldn't say such a thing. Mother and Father died, though they didn't want to. I know you miss them," Theodore said with a sigh. "I miss them too... more than anything. If we can just get to Galenta, to the Borini Queen, maybe she can help us. There must be some way to leave this place."

Minnie poked her brother in the ribs. "We're safer staying here. Aunt Cordelia, she's *worse* than the Vorath. They'd run a mile from her!" Theodore laughed. If nothing else, they were still alive to laugh.

The temperature dropped as they led the horse

through a narrow gully crowded with wild fruit bushes. Blackberries, red-currants, and plump raspberries had the children's mouths watering, but neither dared to stop and forage. Only once they were high up the mountainside, with the afternoon sun on their back, did they risk quickening the pace again.

"Look at that," said Theodore. The road dripped down and rose sharply, offering a stunning view to the west. He and Minnie gazed out over white clay flats stretching into the distance, criss-crossed with stone ridges, rifts and deep, shadowy canyons eroded over the centuries. A vast desert wasteland lay beyond, radiant and deadly, with sweeping sand dunes reaching all the way to the horizon.

The road seemed to go on forever, looping around tight bends and under precarious stone arches, with the terrain becoming more barren with each passing mile. Little survived so far up the mountainside—weary thistles and swarming black flies, mainly. Every sound echoed off the bare rocks, too, their horse's hooves most of all. Potholes like buckets grew wider and deeper where the road ran in a sweeping curve alongside a sheer drop. Any slip or stumble here would be fatal. Jagged boulders and shingle awaited any blundering traveler far below.

"I think this is where the cart wheel broke," said Minnie. "The soldiers were furious, grunting and hitting each other. I had to cover my ears."

"You must have been terrified. How did they fix it?"

Minnie shrugged. "I didn't dare to look. It took most of the day, though. They didn't seem to be in a hurry to get to wherever they were heading. I thought the cart would tip right over the edge the way they were pushing and pulling it around."

"It's a good thing the wheel broke," her brother said, "otherwise, you'd be *miles* away by now."

"That's too awful to even think about," said Minnie, shivering.

Twilight drew in to turn the sky a pale pink. "Hey, look at that," said Theodore. His spirits soared as he spied a silver sliver on the southern horizon, bathed in the last light of day. "It's the ocean. We can't be too far now." For a time, he imagined himself sailing on the waves in a daydream, breathing in the salty air, flanked by dolphins and great grey whales; far away from this awful place.

The horse slowed and came to a gradual halt before long, too weary to carry the children any further. "She's exhausted." Theodore slid down to stroke the mare's long face, swatting away the flies gathered around her eyes.

With a little coaxing, the horse hobbled to a small cove a short way along the road. There she stood with her head bowed low, supping water offered on Minnie's outstretched hands. "Please don't give up on us now, horsey," she whispered. "I promise I'll find you a hundred red apples to eat if you keep going."

"We should rest here for the night," Theodore said,

peering around. "It's too dangerous to go on in the dark. We'll walk right off the edge. It seems safe enough here."

"*Safe!*" Minnie's eyes flashed with fear. "But the Vorath... they'll find us. They'll put me in a cage again. Me and you, Theo." She would rather walk the road blind than ever meet the Vorath again.

Theodore did his best to ease her worries. "I've been looking back all day. I've not seen anyone. We'll be safe tonight." *I hope.*

She remained unconvinced. Minnie leant her head against the horse, silently pleading for the animal to regain her strength, ready to gallop again at the first glimmer of dawn. Eden had already decided the cove would be adequate. The hawk perched herself on a rock jutting out from the wall, dipped her head, and closed her eyes.

Theodore went to explore the cove. Among the crags further back, he found dried scrub, a dead bush, and a few twigs to use as kindling. He used the skills learned from his father to work a small fire to life, allowing the flames to warm his aching body. Minnie left the horse to rest and joined her brother. She wrapped herself in his cloak and curled up beside the fire.

"The stars are pretty here," said Theodore, pointing, but his sister showed little interest. He sat cross-legged, gazing up at the clear night sky, marvelling at the twinkling specks above, when a movement in the crags turned his blood to ice. *It's only the breeze, just the breeze,* he reassured himself.

A black shape took flight from the shadows, invisible against the night, eager to report back to its master. Its wings made hardly a whisper, but the siblings both heard it.

"What was that?" asked Minnie, yawning.

"Just an owl." Theodore looked around anxiously for his spear, angry he hadn't kept it closer to hand. "It's gone now." She didn't need troubling, not after everything she had been through.

He topped up the fire and sat against a rock, cradling his spear and staring out into the darkness. Weariness soon took him, but the nightmares swirling around Theodore's head would bring him no peace whatsoever.

Part 1 · Chapter 11

Avenging the fallen

Tasteless beans and half-a-slice of seeded bread would be their breakfast. It was the only food left to them now. The siblings awoke at first light and ate hurriedly, gulping down their paltry meal with numb, clammy fingers. They set out from the cove on foot with the horse trailing a little further back, still too weak to carry them. For an hour, and then another, the pair trudged south along the road. Black clouds and persistent drizzle soon replaced the warmth that dawn had offered.

"Keep the cloak, Min. You look cold." Theodore pulled it tight around her narrow shoulders. She seemed quiet. "The Borini made that cloak for me, you know. Wait till you see them. They're only this high." He held a hand just below his chest. "Rhal told me that to make the fabric, they dangle down in baskets into deep burrows, gathering silk from a rare plant, or weed... or something like that. Amazing when you think about it."

Minnie forced a smile. She felt tired, and not really in a mood for small talk.

The rain continued to fall and showed little sign of clearing. By midday, however, the road turned south-east and steadily descended, finally delivering the children to the far side of the Aradine Mountains. The sheer drop beside the road faded, too, replaced instead with a steady gravel slope.

A smile came to Theodore's face as he caught sight of more familiar lands. "We made it, Minnie. We made it." He looked up at the mountains and along the rugged foothills below, running for miles to the east and sloping down to overlook the Wilandro Jungle.

Even here, they could hear the waves breaking on the sands of Solar Beach, hidden for now between the boundless ocean and the jungle. The trees and the mountains and the seashore stretched the full length of a stunning coast, all the way to where Galenta, the Borini city lay hidden among the foothills, less than a day's ride to the east. It would take far longer on foot.

"It's beautiful," said Minnie, feeling hopeful for the first time in days.

"Look over there." Theodore jogged forward, oblivious to the churning darkness gathering overhead. "That's the jungle... where the spiders attacked me. Can you see?" *It all looks so small from up here.*

Even the rain failed to dull their spirits. The horse ambled a short way behind with its head pointed to the ground as the siblings tracked east across the foothills, charged with new found energy. Sister and brother skipped along, chatting and laughing like older times.

A sudden, terrified whinny sent an icy shiver through them both. They turned to see the horse stumbling away on four shaky legs. Its eyes were wide, the whites clearly showing.

"Come back," Minnie called out, but the words seemed to only spur the animal on. The rain fell harder and her eyes looked up to see a shadowy vortex of rooks and ravens and a hundred jet-black crows, swirling in the bleak grey sky above. No sooner had she spied the mob, then every bird scattered.

Unease altered to panic when an almighty shriek ripped through the air.

Theodore backed away, unable to comprehend what his eyes were seeing. "What in all the world is *that?*"

The creature appeared around the mountainside, a monstrous wyvern, coated in sleek crimson scales, powering through the rain on huge ragged wings. It shrieked again before swooping down to settle upon the slope nearby. Long, lethal claws gouged at the turf, and the coarse blue spines along its neck quivered.

Minnie's mouth fell open, and all words failed her. *This can't be real,* she told herself. *It's a monster. A real-life monster.* Her face paled further on seeing the menacing warrior mounted in a frayed, high-backed saddle between the beast's wings.

Dismounting, he stood over eight feet tall, with muscle bulging beneath his black leather garb, bound tight with bronze and iron clasps. A rough metallic mask concealed the right side of his face, pinned in place with crude tacks and rivets. He glared at the children through a single milky eye, sunk deep in a wretched, grey-skinned face.

The giant stepped forward in iron clad boots, toying with the enormous battle-axe in his hands. Its double-edged blade held the scars and dints of harrowing deeds that neither sibling dared to visualise taking place. "Do you imagine yourself to be *exempt* from punishment, boy?" the warrior snarled. Rain trickled down an angry scar that ran from mottled forehead to blistered chin, a disfigurement to make even the gentlest creature bitter and tormented.

"Stay back," Minnie squeaked.

He stepped forward again. "Did you truly believe that I would tolerate the slaughter of the soldiers under my command?" Frothy brown phlegm dribbled through a cleft in his lip with each venomous word.

"Who… who are you?" Theodore stammered, edging back.

"The one who brings vengeance to your door. Look at my face, boy," he bellowed. "Look upon the face of Rybas-Kain, the last face your eyes shall ever see again. That, I promise."

The wyvern edged down the hillside on two squat legs, greedily eyeing the children with amber eyes that burned like hot coals. It stooped low to the ground, using the claws at the tip of each folded wing to balance.

Fear had him by the throat. Theodore could scarcely breathe. "We… we didn't mean to harm anyone," he stuttered, looking anxiously from warrior to wyvern. "I… I just wanted Minnie back, that's all. We didn't want to hurt anyone."

"You have chosen your path, *boy*. And your traitorous farmer friend, too. He shall be dealt with in time."

Theodore gripped his spear with both shaking hands, ready to protect his sister against these most terrifying of foes, unsure if his weapon would inflict even a scratch on either. Before he could take another breath, Kain came at him like a demented bull, steaming forward with his axe raised high. Minnie screamed as the blade cut through the air, missing her brother's head by a hair. The warrior lunged again with unnatural speed, and then again, forcing the boy to duck and roll away in desperation, scrambling backwards on his hands and heels through a shallow brook and almost into the wyvern's waiting mouth. Teeth like glass shards snapped shut to almost swallow him whole.

"Back!" Rybas-Kain bellowed at the winged beast. "This one is mine. Do what you will with the girl."

"Leave us alone!" Minnie stumbled back on the wet grass. A clap of thunder boomed overhead to silence her pleas. "Run, Theo!" Wisps of blue-black smoke rose from the wyvern's nostrils as its attention turned on to her.

Kain roared with anger and advanced again, bringing his axe down with such force that it lodged deep into the ground. Thick tendons in his neck flexed like steel wires as he strained to wrench it free. Theodore leapt forward to launch an attack of his own, seizing on the opportunity. It was a fine strike. The edge of his spear crashed against Kain's metal mask to send up a shower of sparks.

"Vermin. How *dare* you think to strike me!" The giant whipped a bone dagger from his boot and surged through the rain, slashing wildly, stalking his wide-eyed prey.

Theodore felt breathless. He stooped and ducked and jabbed as hard as he could at the tough leather armour at his rival's midriff. Rybas-Kain barely flinched. He tore the spear from the boy's hand and snapped the shaft like a twig in a frightening display of dominance, ready to end this tiresome standoff.

Hunter and hunted stood apart, one advancing, one in retreat. *There's nothing I can do,* Theodore told himself. He backed away a little more, fearing for his life.

Thunder exploded and lightning flashed across the sky. The downpour increased, rattling against his arms and shoulders, but just as every shred of hope drained from his body, a distant voice echoed inside his thumping head. *'Be swift. Be strong. Become the difference,'* the voice urged, over and over and over. "The dagger," Theodore whispered. "I need the dagger."

A tormented screech reverberated all around. Eden dived down to gouge at the wyvern's eyes in a blur of wings and claws, desperate to keep the monster away from the girl. It was the bravest act Minnie had ever seen, and the ploy proved to be effective. Incensed at the challenge, the beast gnashed its teeth and launched into the sky to hunt down the maddening bird. Both quickly vanished through the rain and swirling cloud above.

"Fly, Eden! Fly away!" Minnie cried out. She reached down to gather handfuls of mud and pebbles, hurling them through the air to splat against Kain's leather armour. Her actions did nothing but draw his attention.

But the distraction was enough. Theodore drew the crystal blade from his pack and raised it high in his rain-soaked hands.

Rybas-Kain stopped dead in his tracks. His pale eye pulsed with rage. "The Dagger of Shard. That weapon… it vanished an age ago."

The boy stood firm with his jaw tightly clenched.

"How did a worm like you…"

Thunder boomed and a neon streak burst from the heavens with an ear-splitting snap to connect with the blade, spiralling and spitting. Theodore jumped back in shock, almost dropping it to the ground. The crystal absorbed the energy, fizzing and glowing, burning hot and then cold in his hands, though he felt no pain.

"You will give me the weapon *now*, boy!" Kain bellowed.

Theodore's eyes narrowed and fixed on to his enemy's one. "You won't take anything from us," he screamed. "Not today. Not any day. Leave us alone!"

A lance of dazzling white energy burst from the dagger, striking Rybas-Kain flush in the chest. The giant flew back through the air and hit the ground hard, rolling over and over through the grass to settle in a smouldering heap, still and silent.

The children stood quivering, breathing in the reek of scorched iron and leather blowing in the air. Both were utterly stunned.

"What just happened?" Minnie's teeth chattered. Her eyes flicked back and forth between the dagger and Rybas-Kain's crumpled body.

Her brother's heart thumped. "I've no idea." The glow of the crystal steadily dwindled to a flicker and finally faded. "The power... that was *unbelievable*." Theodore gathered up his pack and turned away from the scene. "We need to go, now!"

The youngsters fled together, too afraid to look back,

even for a second.

Part 1 • Chapter 12

An awakening

Fear urged the children on. The afternoon passed by in a flash and still the rain fell. Even under the cover of a hundred leafy cedar trees, even here the downpour found them.

"Keep going, Minnie." Theodore led his sister from grove to grove and across the wind-swept foothills. They charged down to the cliff top as fast as they dared, following the vast arc of the coastline. The Wilandro Jungle grew thick and untamed two hundred feet below them, with every inch drenched in rain.

Minnie's eyes continually scanned the sky for any hint of the wyvern, anxious the beast may descend through the gloom to avenge its master. *Don't come back,* she urged. *Please don't come back.*

They headed east, blundered over gushing brooks and along rocky channels filled with roots and moss, and through shadowy woodland where the branches reached down like grasping wet hands. All the while, rain swept continually down the mountainside on a chill wind to numb their skin.

Within a small cave—in reality, no more than a hollow in a mud bank—the pair took shelter, grateful to have at least some protection from the ever-worsening weather.

"Who was that monster?" Minnie shivered and rubbed her fingers. "I've never been so scared. My heart almost stopped!"

"Mine, too," said Theodore. "Look... my hands won't stop shaking." His arms and legs shook too, partly from the cold, but mostly from shock. "Kain. He said his name was Rybas-Kain."

Minnie kneaded her brother's hands with her own raw fingers. "We're in a living nightmare. And that thing... with the wings. They're not meant to be real. Creatures like that shouldn't even exist! Poor little Eden. I hope she got away."

A normal boy with a normal life would surely have agreed with a shake of their head and a mystified shrug. But after the things Theodore had already seen in his short time on Karadas, he now believed anything to be possible. "This is all wrong. This place... filled with monsters and magic and loathsome savages... we don't belong here."

"No. No, we shouldn't be here," Minnie agreed. "But you were so courageous, Theo. So fearless." She smiled her bravest smile and planted a light kiss on her brother's flushed cheek.

They remained in their hollow for a while, watching the raindrops splash down by their feet. Theodore recounted his night at the eerie fishing village and the tiny island out on the lake where the Guardian's voice had encouraged him to take the crystal blade. Neither could believe the tremendous power it had unleashed, nor did they have any real understanding of its true purpose. "To serve and restore peace to Karadas," Theodore said slowly. "That's what the Guardian's voice said to me."

"How are you supposed to do all of *that*?"

He shrugged, running a finger over the three round notches set in the dagger's bronze cross-guard. "Hopefully, the Borini can help. I'm sure they'll know what to do." Theodore slipped the weapon into his backpack and pulled the drawstrings tight. "Best we keep it hidden until then. It could be a danger to us, too."

Once the rain had thinned slightly, and the pair had thawed somewhat, they abandoned the hollow and set off once again. The dreary foothills were in stark contrast to the tropical scene down below, where the beach stretched along the coast for miles, dotted here and there with craggy black pillars, all edged by the untamed jungle.

Minnie gazed out over the ocean waves as she walked, remembering home and how happy they had all once been as a family. She wiped away a salty tear, recalling their tiny cottage and the welcome fire that would crackle in the hearth. Their doting mother and wonderful father would be there, too, singing and laughing and loving, but not anymore. They were gone now and so was that life; only her brother and the memories remained.

A steep grass bank led the children down towards a dark, dense pine grove, thrusting up beside a towering outcrop of pale rock. Eden swooped down suddenly from the treetops, screeching as they approached.

"Eden!" Minnie cried out, clapping her hands together. "Look, Theo, she made it, she..."

"Quiet." Theodore dragged her to the ground, peering through the long grass.

"What is it?" Minnie whispered. "Is it him?" Her face paled at the thought.

He could see the silvery glint of spears and helms darting between the pines. There were six at least, with one riding upon a glossy black beast. The others were all on foot. "Someone's over there, in the trees. Stay down."

Minnie lay as still as a stone in the grass, holding in a nervy breath. "It's him, isn't it? Or the Vorath... is it the Vorath? Please, Theo, we need to go back."

"It's not them, Min. They're small, really small. It could be the Borini." He crawled forward a little further. "Wait here, let me go and look."

"Theo, no!"

Eden watched on silently from a branch as the boy shuffled along the cliff top, carefully wriggling around weather-beaten bushes and through patches of bottle-green heather, heavy with raindrops. "Over here," he called out unexpectedly, jumping up and waving his arms. "We're over here."

It certainly took the Borini by surprise. They froze at the tree line with their bows and spears poised, peered out through the slots of their grey steel helms with wary emerald eyes.

Minnie had yet to set eyes on a Borini. She summoned her courage and rose to a knee, gazing at the soldiers dressed in burgundy canvas and studded black leather armour. Nor had she seen a Terap. The sight of the oversized stag beetle made her gasp. Its sheer size, black carapace, and sharp mandibles made for a ferocious sight, bringing further dismay to her already-troubled heart.

The Borini remained unmoved. They looked up to the sky and back to the children, muttering to one another in their curious native tongue.

Theodore's initial thrill faded as the Terap wheeled around and galloped away through the trees, kicking up the needles and pinecones littering the floor.

The others circled the children, pointing their spears aggressively and barking commands. Neither Minnie nor her brother understood a single word. When Theodore protested, he earned himself a painful jab in the back to drive him deeper into the woods.

"Who are they?" Minnie asked, reaching for her brother's arm. "They don't seem friendly."

"Borini," he whispered back. "Like Zilic and Rhal. I thought they'd be more pleased to see us."

They came to a halt beside a mossy stone wedge jutting up from the ground, with the soldiers eyeing the siblings suspiciously from the shadows. "I don't understand," Theodore appealed. "It's me, Theodore Reed. If we can speak to Rhal, or the Queen? They know me." Not one of the Borini gave a reply.

It was almost dusk when the Terap returned to the grove, with a second, slightly smaller one arriving a few minutes later.

"Rhal," Theodore cried out. "Thank goodness you're here."

Rhal hopped down and approached the siblings, treading lightly over a carpet of damp pine needles. "How did you get here, Master Theodore?" he asked after an uncomfortable silence. His usually cordial eyes held doubt.

"We came from the lake, along the mountain road," Theodore explained, taken aback at the cautious tone in Rhal's voice. "We made it. I found Minnie. I saved her from the Vorath."

Wind rattled the tree boughs as the Borini whispered to one another. Eventually, Rhal bowed to Minnie, and the soldiers stepped back to stand at ease. "I must apologise for our wariness. It is a surprise to see you here. At sunrise today, our brother Zilicarillion returned. He was alone. We feared you were lost to us."

"Zilic… is alive?" Theodore's eyes welled up as the frightful scene inside the tomb flashed through his mind once again. *That can't be.* "The water… it took him. I was there. I saw it all."

Rhal smiled. "It would take more than a little water to get the best of Zilicarillion. He came to us in a weary state. This is true. It will take many days for him to recover fully, to awaken from the elixir remedy."

"But he will wake up, won't he?" Theodore asked. "He saved my life."

"Put aside your worries, Master Reed. I have been assured that Zilicarillion will make a full recovery. He is among the finest of our warriors, perhaps the finest."

"What about Neup? Is he safe too?"

"Indeed, Neup returned to us in fine health."

Theodore laughed aloud and went to a knee before Rhal, astounded and elated in equal measure. So many questions swirled in his mind, each grappling to be the first for an answer.

As twilight closed in under the trees, all apprehension

and mistrust evaporated. Each soldier stashed their weapons and set about their duties, gathering wood and tending to the Teraps. Two log fires soon burned brightly on either side of the clearing, filling the air with tiny orange embers and a pleasant smoky scent.

Only three of the Borini remained with Rhal once darkness descended fully, with the others continuing up the coast to scout along the cliff top. The children warmed themselves by the fire, sipping hot spiced punch from wooden bowls and listening to the tale of Zilic and Neup, of how they had escaped from the Aradine Path.

"When can we see them?" Theodore asked. He squeezed his sister's hand at the news.

Rhal poked at the coals with the point of a blackened stick. "In time, my friend. For now, Zilicarillion must rest."

In turn, the siblings detailed their journey from the lake. Rhal's face paled upon hearing their account of Rybas-Kain, of how the giant warrior and his crimson wyvern had ambushed the youngsters on the hillside.

"It was my fault," Theodore mumbled. "The soldiers... the herd trampled them when I rescued Minnie. We didn't mean to hurt them."

"But... who is he?" asked Minnie. "He was terrifying."

The Borini bridged his short fingers. "The creature you speak of is known as Rybas-Kain, the Lord and Master to the Vorath. You are both fortunate to have survived, to be here now to tell me this tale. Until this day, his name has only been spoken of in hushed whispers, a phantom that few in these parts believed to even exist."

"Well, he doesn't exist anymore," Minnie grunted. "Theo saw to that."

Rhal shook his head. "I only wish that were true."

"What do you mean?" her bother asked.

"Not three hours past, our scouts saw Kain and his wyvern headed north, over the Aradine Mountains."

Theodore shuddered. "That can't be. He's dead." *He must be dead?*

"The report is accurate, Master Reed." Rhal pointed at a stocky soldier stood across the clearing, honing the point of his spear. "Romizu witnessed the spectacle with his very own eyes: Rybas-Kain slumped forward upon his winged beast, vanishing over the peaks. Injured, he may be, but he lives."

"The dagger, though," said Minnie, "Theo's dagger knocked him to the ground. He didn't get up."

Rhal leant forward. "A dagger, you say?"

The Borini's eyes widened as Theodore brushed the mud from his backpack and reached inside, slowly drawing out the weapon. The crystal blade sparkled in the firelight as he turned it in his hand. "Do you know what this is, Rhal? Rybas-Kain seemed desperate to get hold of it."

Rhal recognised the blade instantly, though he masked his dismay, allowing the children to enjoy their first genuine moment of peace in some time. "Very elegant indeed. On our return to Galenta, we shall certainly try to find out more about it. You have my word. For now though, rest. It has been a trying time for you both." With that, he rose to his feet and bowed, leaving the siblings to their own company. In a little less than an hour, both were fast asleep.

***

Romizu roused the children in the early hours to a waiting meal of foraged nuts, pepper leaves, and a delicious spit-roast rabbit. They brushed the sleep dust from their eyes and ate gratefully, ready to depart on a last hike towards the Borini city of Galenta.

A half-moon watched over the group as they trekked along the clifftop. Theodore and Minnie breathed in the sea air and looked out over the ocean, excited and relieved at the prospect of reaching Galenta, far away from the Vorath and their sinister master, Rybas-Kain.

"If we do get back to England, maybe we *could* still live with the Downings on their farm?" Minnie chattered. "I'm sure they'd take us in. I'd even sleep in the barn. We could work in the yard again and feed the animals, like we did before."

"Maybe. We'll see, Minnie." Their cottage had been on the farmland of the Downing family, who had always been so kind and generous to the Reeds. *I'm sure Aunt Cordelia will have her own ideas,* Theodore considered glumly. The Titanic would surely have docked in New York by now. If the siblings were to somehow make it back to England, to the town of Corsham, perhaps Cordelia might never find out. She may never even know they were still alive. Maybe, just maybe, they could live the dream that Minnie dreamt—a joyful life of peace, back where they had always felt truly safe and happy.

Thin white braids swung gently at Rhal's back as he rode in silence upon his Terap a few paces behind, captured in his own worried thoughts. He could only imagine his Queen's reaction upon hearing that Rybas-Kain was indeed a genuine threat, and that this fabled menace had come so close to their homeland. She had kept her people safe for so long, free from unwanted attention and danger. This news would trouble her greatly.

The grubby backpack slung over Theodore's shoulder made him feel highly uneasy, too. Rhal had claimed to have scant knowledge of the blade when the boy had revealed it, though like a handful of his people, he had heard whispers and rumours regarding the Dagger of Shard and its power. He hoped for the sake of Karadas that the tales were untrue. The thought of bringing such a weapon into the heart of the Borini community weighed heavily upon on his small, rounded shoulders.

***

Dawn broke to the east. The sun rose into a cornflower blue sky, glinting off the ocean and turning the bare rock of the mountains to bronze. It was a radiant new day, perhaps one of last that the inhabitants of Karadas would take delight in. Even the sureness of the sunrise and sunset each day had now become uncertain.

Over a century and a half had gone by since the Dagger of Shard vanished from the realm, lost and forgotten. The Lord and Master to the Vorath, Rybas-Kain, now knew of the blade's existence, witnessing its ominous power first-hand. If this dangerous knowledge were to be uttered in the presence of his own supreme master, and she were to acquire the weapon, the relative peace that much of the realm enjoyed—largely ignored by the enemy—would come to a swift and ruinous end at her hand.

The veiled realm of Karadas would fall into utter chaos, never to be the same again. Under her rule, none would prevail.

Spectre of Destiny

Part 2

Legend of the stones

Part 2 • Chapter 1

Farewell to the realm

It would take more than the afternoon sun to dry the siblings out fully.

"We can try again, Minnie..." Theodore spluttered, wiping the seawater from his eyes with a sandy, wrinkled finger. "Too heavy... the front of the raft was too heavy." Every thread of clothing he wore sagged, thoroughly saturated.

His sister lay beside him on the baking sands of Solar Beach, coughing and equally drenched, with the remains of their wooden raft strewn upon the surrounding shore. Like so many who had tried to break away from Karadas, their attempt had failed. The ocean waves would not let them pass.

***

It had been ten days since the harrowing attack upon the foothills, ten long days since the children's rainy nightmare in the shadow of the Aradine Mountains. The terrifying experience had almost seen the end of them both. Neither Rybas-Kain, nor the crimson wyvern he rode upon, had been seen since. Those who had heard the dramatic tale considered that particular news to be a huge blessing; continued peace in their lives, for a while at least.

The Borini Queen held a deep concern, however. Like most, the name of Rybas-Kain was one of fantasy to her ears, mere gossip, a myth that failed to hold up against reality. "Double the guard duties around the city," she commanded on hearing the report from Rhal, and it was done.

She also ordered scouting parties to scour the foothills to the west, tasked with reporting any hint of a threat. Her warriors travelled east, too, as far as the Reavers' Garrison, an abandoned timber fort built long ago by men. Their kind came to plunder Karadas in the days before the shield—a vast mirage infused with potent magic, veiling the entire realm from the outside world.

A dozen sentries climbed to the highest peaks of

the Aradine Mountains to watch over the land with remarkable brass telescopes. "Set a fire burning at the first sign of danger," she instructed each one. So far, their kindling remained unlit.

Equally worrying was the report that Theodore Reed carried the Dagger of Shard with him. The few Borini that even knew it existed had spoken little and less of the weapon in a century or more. It possessed a tarnished reputation for conflict, pain, and bloodshed, not a subject their people dwelt upon.

"We have worked too hard, and for too long, to jeopardise our peaceful way of life," the Queen announced to her council. "The girl and boy cannot remain here. The risk is too great." She knew full well that Galenta would face a terrible foe and a bleak future should the Vorath discover the ancient blade was concealed within her city.

As both head of the Borini council and chief advisor to his Queen, Rhal had voiced his objection. He promised to learn all that he could about the dagger among the piles of dusty books and crumpled scrolls deep within the vaults of the city library. But at the conclusion of a lengthy discussion, the council voted nine to one against his pleas.

"She can't send us away," Theodore begged when he heard the verdict.

"We've come so far," Minnie added, chewing at her thumbnail.

Rhal calmed the pair as best he could. "Perhaps if you were to appeal directly to the Queen?" he suggested. "I could arrange an audience if you desire?"

The children agreed, though both were nervous on the night of their invitation, fidgeting in their new clothing as they entered the royal chamber. Theodore approached the glowing blue pool at the centre of the throne room dressed in fur-lined leather boots, tight black woollen breeches, and a linen chestnut tunic fastened down the front with five brass clasps. A thick brown belt of gilded leather hugged his waist, studded with silver beads.

Not being a particularly girly girl—more of a tomboy, in truth—Minnie adored her own outfit, pleased to be rid of the fanciful dress that Aunt Cordelia paraded her around in. Her belt and boots and breeches matched her brother's, however, tailors had fashioned her a tunic from soft green leather, finished at the neck and wrists with a gold trim. "Thank you so much," she said to the royal seamstress. She thanked the stylist, too. In true Borini style, her red hair fell forward over her shoulders in two thick braids.

"It is a pleasure to see you again, Theodore Reed," the Queen said from her throne. A Borini youngster plucked delicately at the strings of a silver harp at her side, filling the round, roomy hall with a soothing melody. "It seems I may have underestimated you. You were true to your word, and here your sibling stands."

"I'm still not quite sure how I managed it, your highness."

Minnie bowed her head, too shy to speak. *A real Queen,* she marvelled. *I've seen a Major once, but never an actual Queen!*

Once the pleasantries were over, the rest of the conversation lasted less than five minutes.

Theodore went to a knee when the decree would not be overturned. "But where are we to go?" *You can't send us away,* he wanted to shout. *We came to you for help!*

"We won't be any trouble," Minnie added, finally finding her voice. "We promise."

A sapphire at the Queen's throat glinted as she rose to her feet. "Rest assured, you shall not be abandoned. We have proposed an alternative. Somewhere you shall remain safe and away from danger."

"This way," said Rhal, bowing low. "Follow me."

In the dead of the night, after their leave had been granted, Rhal escorted Theodore and Minnie through the darkened back streets of Galenta and down to a sandy cavern, deep below the royal armoury.

"We can't live here," Minnie grumbled. She eyed a timber trapdoor set in the floor. "There'll be rats and... well, other horrid things."

Dust wafted around the room as Rhal heaved open the trapdoor. "This is merely the entrance," he explained. "From here, a cave network leads away from the city and down to the cliffs overlooking the Wilandro Jungle."

"Rats will be the least of our worries there," Theodore muttered. He ushered his sister down a tiny ladder and followed Rhal along the torch-lit passageway below.

It took almost an hour to reach their destination. A final tunnel led the children into the back of a large wooden shelter attached to the cliffs, crafted from ebony timber and countless lengths of rope. A dozen stout props held the structure in place forty feet up from the ground, just above the jungle canopy.

"This was once a watch post," said Rhal. "Borini scouts kept a constant vigil here during the time of the reavers, to guard against invaders from across the sea. Most of the posts have been dismantled, or have merely fallen into ruin."

Rhal steered the siblings outside and on to a spacious walkway, offering a stunning view over the treetops and the ocean beyond that sparkled in the moonlight. "You shall be safe here," he assured them. "Royal guards shall be close to hand at all times. But please, if you must venture down into the jungle, do so by day, never after dark."

Theodore nodded in agreement, recalling the swarm of gold, crinkled spiders within the canyon. The creatures had almost torn him in two.

It was as homely a dwelling as either could have hoped for. Day after day, the sun beamed down, bright and warm, and cool, gentle winds helped keep the sticky, humid nights at least bearable. Fresh water flowed clear from a crevice beside the walkway, so thirst was never an issue. Provisions of delightful baked bread, hearty broths, and ripe berries in a hundred different colours arrived along the passageway each day from the busy city kitchens. They were never once hungry.

Several rooms were available inside the shelter, but Minnie and Theodore felt safer sharing a single chamber. Swathes of lustrous silk hung from the ceiling and walls, with piles of tiny cotton and fur cushions adding comfort, if enough were gathered.

For several days, with agreeable weather and a spectacular view, both felt settled and content. Eden came to visit Minnie each morning, bringing mice and small pink lizards as a gift for her human friend, much to the girl's dismay. It wasn't long, however, before the itch to return home became overwhelming.

"It is *quite* nice here," Minnie granted. "But I much prefer our cottage. Don't you?"

Her brother shrugged. "The Borini can't expect us to stay here forever."

After a few days, the notion of being away from Karadas took over the children's every thought. They soon discovering a safe path through the jungle, beyond the scant remains of an ancient stone settlement, and down to a secluded clearing close to the ocean. It was here that the siblings planned and set about building a raft to sail away forever.

A year and a month ago, back in England, Theodore

had tried his hand at constructing a small boat of his own, using wood from an old chicken coop. Mr. Downing—who owned the farm where their family once lived—offered the boy as much of the timber as he could carry. He christened his new boat Henrietta, and she made her first and final voyage on Corsham Lake. Theodore returned home that evening soaked and chilled, leaving Henrietta abandoned on the lake bed.

"This one won't sink," Theodore promised his sister. He was excited to succeed this time, relishing the challenge and undeterred by his past failure.

Rhal helped to supply tools and materials, and in only a few short days, the siblings had an impressive raft assembled; five thick logs tethered side by side with strong rope. It even had a mast and a sail.

"It is a fine vessel, my young friends," the Borini remarked on a rare visit to the jungle. "But I fear it will be of little use. Remember my warning, it is..."

"Yes, yes, we know," said Theodore. "It's impossible to leave Karadas by way of the ocean... you've told us a thousand times. We have to try though, you must understand?" *Our raft won't fail,* he thought doggedly. *Our raft will ride over any wave, any wave in the whole wide world.*

"Theo and I don't belong here," Minnie added. "Luck helped us to escape the Vorath, and fend off that brute, Rybas-Kain. But our luck will run out soon."

Rhal bowed. "You have earned your right to try, my friends. This is true. Please do take care, though. The ocean waves will be persistent."

"I've hidden the dagger," Theodore groaned, straining to bind an extra length of rope across the bow. "It's under the main passageway leading into the shelter, the third tile back... just in case."

The Borini felt troubled but kept his composure. Rhal knew the realm would be a safer place with the weapon far away across the ocean, to never fall into the wrong hands. But he could ask no more of the youngsters.

"Will you say goodbye to Zilic?" Theodore asked. He held up a hand to shield his eyes from the midday sun. "I've still not been able to see him, to thank him. He and Neup saved my life."

"I will do as you ask," Rhal said with a smile. "Zilicarillion will know."

"Farewell then, Rhal. Thank you for all you've done. We'll always remember you."

Minnie crouched low to hug their tiny friend. "Thank you, Rhal. You've been so kind." Her black leather boots creaked lightly as she rose.

An hour on, Rhal had returned to Galenta, and the raft was ready to set sail. One colossal danger still remained, however: Rakista, the beast of Solar Beach. Theodore had encountered the monster on his arrival to Karadas. Even a momentary thought of that day caused him to shiver.

"We have to be certain," he insisted. "Rakista's a lot faster than it looks."

They watched patiently from the undergrowth. Only once they were convinced that the coast was clear did they dare to begin. Excitement and trepidation swept through their veins as they burst through a curtain of tacky, limp leaves, with Theodore dragging their raft along a trail of greasy kelp and down toward the waves that crashed and thumped upon the shore.

Minnie came behind, dragging makeshift oars, food, and water, for what would surely be a lengthy trip. "Out of the way," she cried at the gulls probing at the sand up ahead. They scattered to the sky in a flurry of shrieks and feathers as the raft hurtled towards them. Eden dug her talons into the mast, ignored the gulls to keep her glossy, black eyes fixed on the ocean.

"Get ready," Theodore cried. "We're almost there… this is it!"

A powerful wave immediately hit the raft to soak them through. Theodore and Minnie leapt up on to the deck to secure various pouches, boxes, and packs into position with ropes and leather straps. They took an oar each and rowed with all their strength, desperate to escape the powerful current. Tense minutes passed, buffeted by the surf. Time, as well as the raft, seemed to stand still. But finally, after what felt like an age, they made headway, edging away from the beach and between colossal rocks encrusted with barnacles.

Minnie let out a nervy laugh. "We're moving. Theo, we're moving!"

"It's working!" her brother yelled. "Keep rowing."

The raft crept further out, riding the sun-soaked waves that seemed utterly determined to force them back. Before their eyes, the sand and the trees, the foothills and the rocky peaks of Karadas all faded steadily from view, concealed under a magical mirage of sea, cloud, and sky.

"Keep going," cried Minnie, driving her oar deep into the water. Her muscles burnt and salt water stung her eyes. The pain was excruciating, but she could not rest. *Keep going, keep rowing,* she chanted silently. *Keep going, keep rowing.*

Ill-fated groans from the raft did little to ease their nerves. Eden abandoned the mast as it rocked from side to side, forward and back. Incredibly, the further away from Karadas they ventured, the larger and more violent the waves became. Waves that had felt like steep hills until now were becoming more like small mountains, steering the raft up and down at precarious angles.

The siblings were cruelly exposed to the elements, suffering the full chill of icy sea spray and the bite of the fierce ocean winds, summoning back the troubled memories of their last terrible experience upon the waves. Those fateful nights aboard the Titanic's lifeboat felt like half a lifetime ago now.

Theodore's hands felt raw and his teeth chattered uncontrollably. "Minnie, hold on!" *Please, no. Not again.* He watched on in dread as a tremendous swell of sea water rose up, ready to roll over the raft. "Hold on!"

The wave struck hard, breaking the deck apart as if they had crafted it from straw. Brother and sister floundered in a white froth, struggling to keep above the surface, desperate to seize any part of their ruined craft. Anxious minutes passed, pulled and jostled, stunned and nauseous as the horizon pitched one way and then the other.

Minnie arrived back to the shore first with her hair tangled with seaweed, clinging to a shattered section of the mast. Her brother appeared soon after, carried up the beach on two logs that had somehow remained tethered.

Neither could summon a single word for a time. They lay sprawled on the sand, contemplating Rhal's warning. Over the years, many had tried to sail away, but all had failed. Clearly, the siblings would not be leaving the veiled realm of Karadas any time soon.

Part 2 • Chapter 2

Hateful recollections

Far past the Aradine Mountains, over rivers and fields and valleys, beyond vast forests and bottomless lakes, as far north as the realm of Karadas extended, a round, windowless tower stood half in ruin, steadily sinking into the surrounding marshland.

No sane person ever came to this place. Few had the audacity to even utter its name. Even then, the bleak province known as the Grey Fangs would be spoken in a murmur, on a muffled breath. His own wyvern had shrieked in terror as they approached, leaving Rybas-Kain to walk the last half mile alone. "Cowardly beast!" he had raged, although his own courage now eked away with every painful step.

He approached from the south under an empty sky as dark as ink, devoid of even a single star. Kain lurched towards the tower on unsteady legs, using the handle of his huge battle-axe to keep himself from toppling over, sloshing through filthy mud pools that threatened to suck the boots from his sizeable feet. His own disfigured face served as a reminder of the horrors he had once suffered here.

Since his defeat upon the foothills, cast down by the Dagger of Shard, Rybas-Kain had hidden himself away, seeking a solitude at the Vale of Ashes, a mountainous region of blackened rubble and noxious gas plumes, ravaged centuries ago by a volcanic cataclysm.

Days and nights followed, reeling in agony from his wounds. Eventually, Kain submitted to the inevitable conclusion: his message must be delivered, whatever the cost to himself. "There is no other choice," he muttered grimly. "I must go to her."

That one decision, to come here to Grey Fangs, now felt like a rash choice. The breeze died down as he stepped beyond a ring of oval runestones encircling the tower, halting at the edge of a broad moat brimming with water as dark and viscous as oil. Kain gazed into a darkened doorway at the base of the tower with his one good eye, milky and bloodshot as it was. The other eye saw nothing, concealed under a metallic mask pinned to the right side of his face.

"Master," he called out, taking a knee. "Master... your servant has come before you." Silence answered him. "Master, I..."

The moat quivered and burbled, and the air filled with the stink of rotting corpses. Rybas-Kain snapped his head to one side as a dazzling ruby glow burst from the doorway. Bats came too, spiralling up and around the tower to vanish into the blackness above. He peered between the fingers of a scorched leather glove to see a shimmering silhouette glide forward, hovering a few inches above the water.

"Tell me, creature," a husky female voice uttered, full of scorn and laced with an exotic accent. "Why are you here?"

"Forgive me, Master," Kain stammered, dribbling with each nervy word. "That which you seek, the Dagger of Shard. Master, it has arisen."

After a strangling silence, she spoke. "And you have the blade with you?"

A bowed head served as his answer.

"Why do you come here, only to utter empty words?"

"Master, it is in the possession of a great warrior. I was taken unawares... the Dagger of Shard shall be yours once again. I promise."

The moat boiled. "You forget, my decrepit creation. I see your mind. I see all of your many, *many* lies." A rumble rolled through the night sky.

Kain went to both knees, every inch of his eight-foot frame reduced down to that of a cowering wretch. A silvery fog swept over the moat from the doorway and the water turned still. His eye widened as a faint vision played out upon the surface, an apparition of the recent past.

"A great warrior, you say. I see only a weak human boy."

"There were others, they..."

"Ah, yes, there she is," the voice mocked, "a spindly little girl. More than capable of turning the tide of battle, I do not doubt." The fog cleared, and the moat boiled again. "Have you grown so feeble?"

He gave no answer. His own mind had betrayed him, his failings laid bare in the water. A bolt of ice-white lightning burst from the darkness overhead to strike the crumbling merlons at the top of the stone tower, sending down a shower of gravel and dust. When Kain looked again, the silhouette had vanished; only the darkened doorway remained.

Rybas-Kain levered himself up using his axe and backed away, fearful of the punishment his lies and inadequacy would surely incur. He turned from the tower and stumbled towards the camp in the distance up ahead, glaring into the gloom on either side. A dozen large fires burned red and gold and yellow to turn the horizon into a fiery dawn. The smell of roasting meat grew stronger as he approached; the reek of smelting iron and steel even stronger still.

The camp spread far and wide, where his army of tall, wiry Vorath hurried back and forth between the fires to carry out their tasks. Huge black shapes moved, too, laden with cargo and heaving great timber war machines that creaked and groaned. The clank of hammers could be heard, as well as the snarls and shrieks of dangerous, scaly beasts being tamed in their cages. The Vorath were his to command, every one of them, though not one of them had anything but a deep hatred for him.

A whisper at his shoulder turned him back around. The tower remained black, almost lost against the night. Rybas-Kain dropped to his knees as an icy gale swept forward, stinging the exposed skin of his face and driving the air from his lungs.

"Was I wrong to recruit you?" The husky voice seemed to be everywhere as it spoke in harsh tones. Everywhere, yet nowhere. "Are you still the one to lead this rabble of wretched creatures?"

"I live to serve you," Kain shrieked, utterly terrified.

The wind dwindled to a light breeze. "No more. This realm has revelled in my kindness for too long. All of their miserable lives exist only because I allow it."

Only when he was certain the voice had finished did Rybas-Kain dare to speak. "What do you command of me, Master?"

A rumble rolled through the night sky. "Now is the time. Let it begin."

Part 2 • Chapter 3

A royal visit

Only a few supplies remained from their failed sea voyage. The children trudged through the undergrowth carrying their belongings under their arms and over their shoulders, on and on towards their temporary cliff-side home; now, it seemed, their permanent home. A far-off bellow from Rakista along the coast had hurried their retreat into the jungle.

"There must be another way to get home," Minnie pondered, hopping over a narrow brook. "We can't be stranded here. Not forever and ever and ever."

"Our next raft needs to be bigger," said Theodore. "Much bigger. And we need to make sure the logs are..."

The sight of a hooded figure up ahead stopped them in their tracks. He stood below a crumbed stone archway clad in thick brown vines. The stranger walked towards them, flicking back the hood of his grey cloak at the last moment.

"Zilic!" Theodore cried out. He dropped his cargo and rushed to embrace his tiny friend. "It's wonderful to see you. Minnie, look... it's Zilic. He's here."

She was still quite amazed at how small the Borini folk were—barely reaching up to her brother's chest. Minnie smiled kindly. "Thank you, Zilic. We owe you everything."

Zilic bowed gracefully. His emerald eyes shone above a button nose in a round bronze face. "You are most welcome, my dear. I only wish I had been there to help with the rescue. Although I hear Master Reed handled the situation rather well."

A blush spread over Theodore's cheeks and Minnie burst into a fit of giggles. Their joy turned to bewilderment when a procession of Borini warriors emerged through the undergrowth dressed in royal blue suits and grey steel half-helms. The soldiers stepped aside in unison to create an aisle of leather, shield, and spear, allowing their Queen to approach, robed in a sleek amber gown. Rhal stood at her side, visibly pleased to see the youngsters had survived their brief but eventful ocean adventure.

"Your highness," Theodore bowed, surprised to see the Queen away from the safety of her city.

"We are delighted at your return," the Queen said in an enchanting voice, as a pair of lavender butterflies fluttered around her shoulders. Today, she wore a delicate chain at her neck, matching the silver band resting upon her bronzed, hairless head. "It seems that our realm may not be done with you yet. All for the good. We have unearthed knowledge that we wish to share with you both."

Rhal stepped forward and peered into the trees. "Let us return to your dwelling, young friends, away from hidden eyes and ears."

A hush fell over the jungle as the soldiers used scythes and wooden staffs to widen the path back toward the cliffs. They marched up a steep ramp and on to the wooden walkway attached to the rock face. Each of their boots stepped in perfect time. Minnie rushed forward, eager to tidy their makeshift home. *It's such a mess.* She had not imagined they would return, let alone have royalty come to visit.

Servants arrived down the tunnel soon after with all manner of supplies, setting up chairs and stools around a low oval table, along with bowls of figs and sugared plums. Three stone braziers were lit in the clearing below, warming the walkway above and filling the air with a light charcoal aroma.

As the afternoon turned to evening and the birds throughout the jungle sang their last songs of the day, Theodore went to recover the Dagger of Shard, placing it at the centre of the table. The Queen gazed at the ancient weapon, mesmerised.

Rhal cleared his throat and produced a worn canvas scroll from the sleeve of his silvery gown. The scroll bore an image of the curved dagger in cracked oil paint, with text and queer glyphs scribed in fine black ink below. "After many hours of searching, I discovered this parchment deep within the city library."

"Can you read the words?" asked Theodore. "What do they say?"

The Queen leant forward to point out several strange symbols. "The writing is in a language we are not fluent in. But there are clues."

"A trio of Warlocks, both wise and powerful, once lived at the age-old shrine known as Alkan," Rhal went on. "That much we had heard. However, we have since discovered from long-forgotten records that the Warlocks and the Guardians, whom they once tutored, began a destructive conflict."

"What was their dispute?" asked Zilic, hearing the tale for the first time.

"The Dagger of Shard," the Queen muttered, turning to face Theodore. "We do not know which race crafted the blade, but it would appear to have been created to seize overall power throughout the realm. The Warlocks and Guardians fought, but both are now only a memory. Neither has graced Karadas in one hundred years or more. Tell me again, my dear, how did the blade come to you? You spoke of a voice."

Darkness claimed the jungle as Theodore described his night upon the lake, recounting the strange hoop of green flame upon the water and the slanted rock islet at its centre. It had been here that the Guardian's voice had freely offered him the dagger. Even now, it was hard to recall the episode fully. "I don't remember the exact words. It felt more like a dream. A voice spoke to me. It claimed to be a spirit; a spirit of Zell-Ku."

"The Guardians, as a group, were known as the Zell-Ku," Rhal explained to Minnie. "They were celebrated protectors of the realm. Master Reed, what else do you recall?"

"About becoming the difference... and a sea tower. That was it. He said to seek the tower. It's somewhere near a desert. At least I *think* that was it." *This all sounds so foolish now,* he reflected. His cheeks reddened. *I must sound like I've gone dotty!*

Zilic and Rhal exchanged a glance as a host of glow bugs mingled with the rising embers to create a wondrous light show. All were silent in thought.

"There is only one tower that I know of near here," said Rhal, "but it fell to the ground long ago."

"Up on the plateau," Zilic nodded. "I have seen the ruin from afar. At the edge of the Jurkoon Desert, close to..."

"The Jurkoon Desert, that was it!" Theodore interrupted,

clicking his fingers. "That must be the one."

"Well, we may have one piece to our puzzle," Rhal chuckled.

"What are these?" asked Minnie, pointing to three circular marks on the parchment, each a faded colour of green, blue, and crimson.

"Crystal stones. Or gems, each with an energy, a strength. At Alkan, the Warlocks guarded one stone each." Rhal pointed to the green circle. "As far as we understand, they named this one life, or Earth. Master Reed, look at the hilt of the dagger. Do you see the hollows in the cross-guard? Three hollows to hold the three gemstones, to harness their combined power."

Theodore ran his fingers over the blade, imagining how the gem stones would look set in the bronze cross-guard. *Combined power... but power to do what?*

"What are the other two called?" Minnie asked nervously, tapping her heels against her chair. "What do they do?"

"For now, that remains a mystery," said Rhal. He rolled the scroll delicately and popped it back into his sleeve. "I shall continue in my search, however. There are still many vaults to explore in the library."

The Queen stood and smoothed down her dress. "The blade is a complication we did not envisage, but it seems to have come to you for a reason." Her eyes fell upon Theodore again. "I believe you are here, on Karadas, for a purpose. However, the Dagger of Shard cannot remain here. Each day, it threatens to bring grave danger to our people. If a Guardian still exists by some means, even in spirit, he will surely know what must be done."

Without a command, the soldiers snapped to attention, ready to escort their Royal Highness back to the city. "Zilicarillion, you will guide Theodore Reed to the sea tower. Learn all that you can. You will travel at first light."

Zilic bowed. "It shall be done, Your Highness."

"But we just want to go home," Theodore protested. "I never wanted this."

The Queen made her way to the rear of the shelter to leave only the sweet peachy scent of her perfume behind. She and her warriors vanished into the passageway, with their footfall steadily echoing to silence.

Rhal stepped forward before joining them. "If it is home you seek, away from this realm, a Guardian may know a way. If he still lives, that is. Along with the Warlocks of old, their knowledge was said to be beyond compare. I wish you good fortune, my friends." He bowed low to leave the siblings and Zilic alone.

"I'm going with you," said Minnie. "I won't stay here alone."

"And I won't leave you." Theodore hugged his sister. "If Rhal thinks this is our best chance to get away from here, we *have* to take it. This could be our only hope. We have to try." *We have to.*

"The plateau we seek is to the west of this very jungle," Zilic explained, looking along the darkened cliff face, "where the Aradine Mountains reach down to touch the ocean. The plateau forms a barrier between the sands of Solar Beach and the Jurkoon Desert beyond."

"Are you well enough, Zilic?" asked Theodore. "To make the journey, I mean?"

"I am indeed, my friend. Thank you for your concern."

"We didn't want to end up carrying you," Theodore added, forcing a smile. "How far is it?"

"A day's hike, no more. Have no fear. Together, we shall find your Guardian. Before we leave, there are arrangements I must make. Try to rest. Be ready at sunrise." Zilic bowed and took his leave, hurrying into the passageway to catch up to Rhal.

Neither Minnie nor Theodore slept much that night. Dreams of home crowded any rest they managed: visions of the cottage they had lived in as a family back in England, happier times that would never return. Sickness had taken their mother and father only six months past, a tragedy that left their world turned upside down. If they could somehow get home to Corsham, would the Downing family welcome them back to live on their farm again? Would Aunt Cordelia let them? So many questions. Too few answers.

***

As promised, Zilic returned as the sun rose, smouldering across the ocean waves to the east. Neup arrived with him, loaded with water and food supplies for the journey. Blankets and kindling, too, as well as the essentials for a simple canvas shelter, should the need for sanctuary arise. The giant stag beetle carried the extra weight with ease.

Neup clicked excitedly at seeing Theodore again, pushing forward to nuzzle the boy's hands gently with two sharp mandibles and bristling antennae, eyeing the children through round black eyes the size of freshly minted sovereigns. Although Minnie held a great affection for almost any animal, the Terap's daunting features inclined her to keep a safe distance.

"For you," said Zilic. "This one should be far more comfortable." He handed Theodore a seamlessly tailored cloak woven from turquoise silk, without so much as a loose thread visible—unlike the hurriedly fashioned garment Rhal had provided many days ago.

Minnie beamed as Zilic handed her a matching, slightly smaller cloak.

"These are also for you. They were crafted a few days past at Rhal's command." He unfurled a beige canvas sheet and presented each sibling with an oak bow polished to a shine with beeswax; a quiver of feathered arrows accompanied each weapon.

"Thank you," Theodore and Minnie said in unison, though her brother's reply held far more excitement than her own.

"I shall teach you the skill as time allows, although I hope for all of our sakes that they shall not be required. Now, if you are ready, we shall begin. To avoid unwanted attention, our path shall be through the jungle, keeping close to the shore."

"Good idea," said Minnie. "Then no one will see us from up on the cliffs."

"*And* we avoid Rakista," Theodore added. "That's important."

"Indeed. Very good, my friends, you learn fast."

With their new weapons slung over opposite shoulders, the siblings followed Zilic through the Wilandro Jungle. The first hour of their journey felt effortless, almost enjoyable. Minnie counted several species of birds and butterflies along the way, each a more vibrant colour than the last. The following hours were far less pleasant. Persistent rain rattled down, and the undergrowth altered to a thick, wild tangle. Even with his great strength and burly jaws, Neup struggled to make much headway through the stubborn wall of plants. By noon, each of them was caked in mud, grazed, and weary. They were going nowhere fast.

Zilic, usually so mild tempered, soon lost all patience. "We will be in this infernal jungle for all eternity. South, we must head to Solar Beach," he announced. "If we keep to the shadows, we should go unnoticed."

"*Should?*" cried Theodore, spinning around. He was in no rush to be near Rakista ever again. "It's too dangerous." *This is madness!*

"I know the beast and how it hunts. We shall be safe."

It took until late afternoon to retrace their steps and find a suitable path to the coast. By then, the rain fell in thick vertical drops, hammering the leafy canopy above. Minnie and Theodore toiled in silence behind Neup, cold and fearful, wrapped tightly in their new silk cloaks.

The rain ceased as the group approached the seashore. They could find no trace of Rakista. Any tracks the monster may have left upon the sand that day were gone, washed away by the downpour.

Zilic stepped out from the tree line to make certain the beach was clear. "We have good fortune, my friends. Come, stay close. We should reach the sea tower by dusk."

They trudged along the shore for what felt like hours, continually turning to make sure that Rakista had not sneaked up on them. Dark obsidian pillars dotted the sand along the way, glimmering with powerful magic. The children had counted thirty-two of them by the time they caught their first glimpse of the plateau.

It stood like a wall across the sand, weather-beaten and riddled with cracks, reaching fifty feet into a dusky evening sky. White waves thumped against its base where it stretched out into the ocean, and in the opposite direction, the plateau disappeared through the jungle before slanting up to blend with the foothills high above.

Minnie shivered. A sudden chill passed through her body. "It was here... I remember this place," she stammered, peering through the growing gloom. "The Vorath, they captured me here..."

"You're safe, Minnie. You're safe." Theodore gripped her tightly. "They're not here now."

She leant on her brother's shoulder, and her eyes gently closed. Immediately, they sprung open again. *What in the world is that?* Minnie froze, too afraid to scream, watching a gigantic black shadow lumber along the beach at their back. It came almost silently through the twilight haze, a monstrous silhouette set against a sky of blood-red clouds.

Despite all of their careful planning, Rakista had found them.

"Run!" cried Zilic. He leapt up to the saddle on Neup's back, sending a hail of arrows toward the beast.

A hundred birds fled from the treetops as Rakista roared, a bellow so deep the siblings felt it in their bones. Theodore gripped his sister's hand, and they fled along the beach, wide-eyed and petrified.

The sand around their feet shook as the creature followed, flexing two clawed hands and chomping needle-sharp teeth in anticipation of the meal to come.

Theodore reached the plateau first, breathing hard, desperate to find a place to hide or a ledge or a nook to climb up. He found none of those things. The children stood with their hands flat against the cooling rock. An unbearable sense of peril washed over them both. Their end had surely come. They could only watch on in dread as Rakista drew closer.

Part 2 • Chapter 4

Downfall

"This way... hurry!" Zilic beckoned frantically to the siblings where the sea met the sand along the plateau.

The beast approached, glaring at the children with wet black eyes that flickered cold and cruel. Pointed teeth opened and closed, and its great clawed hands flexed again.

Minnie dashed across the sand, impelled by terror, hurdling heaps of rotting kelp gathered upon the shore. Wet sand sucked at her boots as she ran.

"In here," Zilic cried. "Get inside. Go! Go!" He vanished into a narrow crack in the plateau, edged with barnacles and gloopy black slime. There was no chance the Terap would fit inside. Neup latched on to the rock-face with six barbed feet and clambered up and away from danger.

Rakista's cloven hooves thumped on the beach.

Sister, then brother, dived headlong into the crack, scrambling forward on their hands and knees through the sand and splintered seashells, moments before a massive, gnarled fist clattered the rock-face.

"Move!" Theodore screamed. "Go, get further in."

Rakista smashed the plateau again and again, shaking it to the foundations. *Thud. Crack. Boom.* Then silence.

"Wait," Minnie whispered. She lay perfectly still, listening to the salt water washing through the stone and gravel piled high at the entrance.

"We're... we're trapped," Theodore stammered. He could see nothing in the darkness. "How do we get out?"

Zilic remained calm. "Patience, my friend. I shall search for an exit."

"There's no time for patience," Minnie cried. "The tides coming in!" The ocean came steadily at first, and then more rapidly, moving up her legs and on to her body. Her hands scrambled blindly through the sand, grating against the tips of her soft fingers.

"Keep moving," Theodore spluttered, utterly shocked at the swift rise of the tide. "Where's Zilic?"

"I don't know... I can't see anything." Minnie flinched as a white light flashed and a tiny gloved hand gripped her wrist, dragging her up and into a cramped, circular hollow above. She thrashed her legs, desperate to grip on to the slimy rock.

"Where is Master Reed?" Zilic clung to the wall further up with a small, bright lantern swinging from his leather belt.

Theodore burst through the surface a second later, drawing in a sharp, thankful breath to fill his empty, aching lungs.

"We almost *drowned* in there!" his sister cried out, heaving a thick scarf of brown seaweed from her shoulders. "Too close… that was too close."

"The water will not stop here," the Borini urged. "We must climb, fast."

As if the ocean had overheard his warning, sea water surged up the shaft with incredible force, thrusting the children and Zilic up with it, pushing and jostling them against the rounded stone walls to launch them into the air like a trio of champagne corks.

The companions floundered in a puddle of foam and brine on the plateau's summit under the glimmer of a low, hazy moon, with coughs and groans and splutters as their only conversation for a minute or more.

"That's certainly *one* way to get up here," a friendly voice chuckled.

A second Borini stepped forward from behind Neup and slipped a large backpack from his shoulder. He looked to be slightly taller than Zilic, with a scarlet leather patch concealing his left eye. The other glowed bright emerald in the darkness. A thick plait of white hair tumbled down his back to brush the heels of two black boots. "Your obsession with adventure will catch up to you one day, nephew."

"Hopefully not on this day." Zilic brushed himself down and the two Borini bowed low to one another. They wore near-identical outfits: grey woollen cloaks, light leather, and gilded steel armour at their chest and shoulders. "May I introduce my uncle, Olenious," he said to the children. "He has been both my bane and mentor for many a year."

Theodore smiled at seeing the two of them together, recalling how fondly Zilic had spoken of Olenious during their ill-fated journey through the Aradine Path; of the taunts and japes the pair continually shared.

"Your uncle?" said Minnie. "But you look the same age."

"You are very kind, Princess." Olenious walked forward and placed a hand on his nephew's shoulder. "Zilicarillion has not aged well. This is true."

That made the siblings laugh. It was the first time they had ever seen Zilic look abashed, though the younger Borini took the jest rather well.

"Thank you, Uncle, for your warm words. Now, if you would allow us to focus back on our task." Zilic turned to peer along the plateau, to where the rugged tip jutted out over the ocean.

"I was expecting you sooner, Zilicarillion. My scouts

and I were making our descent from the mountains when word reached me of your quest. I came at once."

"Did you see any Vorath?" Minnie blurted, fearful of the answer. "Or him?"

"We are free from unwanted eyes," said Olenious. "Borini troops are watching the foothills above, even as we speak. At present, there has been no sight of the enemy on our side of the Aradine Mountains. Nor their master. Though I see you managed to find a monster of your own."

"Rakista!" Theodore cried out, suddenly remembering. He rushed to the edge of the plateau to see wave upon wave rolling and crashing on to the sand down below, but he could see no sign of the beast.

"We are safe up here," Olenious reassured him. "Rakista may be formidable on the sand, but even his great strength cannot scale sheer rock."

The relief on Theodore's face was clear to see. He had escaped Rakista's grasp on two occasions now. A third encounter would surely end very differently.

"Just in case," said Zilic, "I suggest we find what we are looking for and be off this rock as swiftly as possible."

Their search was brief. They found blocks of bleached white stone along the plateau where the Guardian's tower had once stood, scattered among the ferns and brittle, windswept grass.

"Over here," Theodore called to the others. He handed

his bow and quiver to Minnie and heaved a stiff bushel of heather aside to reveal a gloomy staircase descending into the plateau. A carpet of black moss clung to each step. "This must be it."

"Hard to believe this was once a great sea tower," said Olenious. He took Zilic's lamp and circled the stairwell twice. His cloak flapped like a moth's wings in the brisk ocean wind. "It is one of many that once stood around Karadas. What a glorious sight it would have made in its day."

"It's just a ruin," Minnie muttered. *There can't be anyone living here?*

Zilic stepped down and sparked a second lantern into life. "Wait here with Neup. We shall return soon."

Theodore followed before his sister could object. Their shadows trailed behind them until they merged into the darkness below.

"Let the boys go and play," said Olenious. "Come Princess, a hot meal and a warm fire would be a blessing to us both."

In the bowels of the plateau, a sturdy iron door stood closed at the foot of the stairs, heavily corroded by time. A pattern swirled across its surface, created from strands of silver and cracked copper wire, finished with rouge and jade pearls. To the touch, the door held a deep, unnatural chill.

"It's locked," Theodore whispered. He poked and

prodded, running his fingers around the joints of the frame in search of a handle or secret catch.

Zilic checked lower down. "Here, Master Reed." He swept away a build-up of sand and grit at the base of the door and pointed to a discreet slot. "Place the tip of the dagger in here."

The crystal blade shimmered expectantly as Theodore knelt. His hands shook and his heart raced as the dagger slid into the groove with surprising ease. He and Zilic stepped back to see the decorative seal on the door come alive, lit by an unseen force. They stared in amazement. A vibrant image flickered before their eyes; a tumbling ocean, with a hundred glittering stars and coloured comets above.

Ever so slowly, the gate rose into the ceiling, rumbling, as iron scraped against stone. Theodore retrieved the dagger from the key slot and placed it into his backpack. "How did you know it would open?" he asked, peering into the darkness beyond. *Every day stranger than the last.*

Zilic shook his head and shrugged. "Purely a guess."

A tall passageway lay ahead with slanting walls clad in blue and ruby tiles, leading down into a chilly, three-sided chamber. They entered together. Step by step, the temperature dipped and a musty smell grew. In the lamplight, their breaths appeared as puffs of ghostly fog. A faded mosaic covered the entire floor, partly hidden under a fine layer of salt and sand, and at the back of the chamber, ocean spray blew in through a gaping hole where a section of the wall had collapsed. Faint stars could be seen between the clouds, winking in the night sky.

"This is incredible," said Theodore, marvelling at the stone shelves to their left, crammed with decaying leather books, coiled scrolls, and countless glass jars brimming with peculiar coloured liquids. Thick dust and cobwebs covered every item.

Zilic moved to the opposite wall to inspect three oval hollows carved into the rock. Each one was five feet wide and twice that in height. Two were veiled in shadow, but from the third, a dim orange glow pulsed gently from dark to light, then light to dark. "Look here." Yet even as he spoke, the light faded to black, and vanished.

Minnie was right, Theodore thought. *This place is a ruin.* "There's nothing here, Zilic." His hopes of ever finding the Guardian faded, as did any dream of him and his sister ever returning home. He kicked at the floor and huffed. "It's all been a waste of time.

Zilic whirled around at the sound of a sharp tap on the floor behind them, wood on stone. In a flash, he unsheathed his twin silver daggers, poised to defend, prepared to attack.

Even to the eyes of a Borini, the sight was incredible.

A slender figure stood tall in the shadows, exuding authority and robed in a white canvas shawl. He gazed at his two visitors with pale watery eyes above a narrow, aquiline nose in a blanched, time-worn face.

"We come here in peace... to seek knowledge," Zilic said in a shaky voice, dropping to a knee. "Are you truly a Guardian of Zell-Ku?"

Theodore watched on nervously, dismayed to see Zilic so full of fear. He had only ever known the Borini warrior to act with courage and resilience, whatever the threat. "I was told to come here," he added in an equally daunted tone. "On the lake... in the night. Was that your voice?"

The Guardian gave a subtle nod. He leant on a bowed sepia staff and moved stiffly towards the crumbled wall to look out over the ocean. A sea breeze blew in to ruffle his drooping, silvery moustache and strands of snowy hair sprouting from an elongated head, flecked with light brown freckles. "The waves. Can you hear their song?" he said. His voice resonated, deep and enchanting.

"I can hear the waves," Theodore replied. *He looks almost human,* he thought, but kept the notion to himself.

"Long have I yearned to the listen to the music of the ocean again."

"We have the weapon," said Zilic after an uncomfortable silence. "The Dagger of Shard. We return it to you."

The Guardian turned his head and smiled, gripping his staff with both hands. "The Dagger was not, and never shall be, mine. It is of Warlock craft, forged by the head of their order. Thankfully, it is now in the safe hands of the boy."

Theodore felt for the curved blade through his backpack, hesitant to reveal it. *He's blind. I don't think he can see.*

"You are perceptive, Theodore Reed," the Guardian said, meeting the boy's gaze. "My sight has dimmed, but I still possess the vision of my mind. I can sense your thoughts at this very moment, young one. All of your dreams and hopes and desires... the distant call of a faraway land."

"That's all we want... my... my sister, me and Minnie," Theodore stuttered. *How can he know this?* "We don't belong here. Is there a way to leave?"

"When Karadas is at peace." The Guardian turned again to face the ocean. "Of late, a poison has spread over the land. Left unchecked, the realm shall be forsaken. You, Theodore Reed, *you* must become the difference."

"I don't understand? Why me? Where would I even begin? There must be someone else..."

"Once Karadas is at peace. When the Dagger of Shard and the Zeon Stones are one, Master Reed, then, and only then, shall the desire you thirst for be quenched."

"Home, with Minnie?" *I'll do whatever it takes,* he vowed. *I will... I have to.*

"Come, hold out your hands. Let my mind link with your own."

Theodore approached the Guardian once Zilic had nodded his approval, offering up his shaking hands.

"What will I see?" he asked.

"Everything, Theodore Reed. Everything." The Guardian muttered unknown words and laid his wooden staff across the boy's quivering palms.

A shiver ran through Theodore's body, from the flats of his feet to the hair on his head. Eyes that had been blue his entire life turned to matte black orbs as knowledge flowed into his mind. The two were one.

Zilic looked on in wonder. Streaks of white light encircled the Guardian and the boy, coiling one way and then the other, spiralling around their arms and legs like a hypnotic haze.

But the Borini's wonderment twisted instantly to deep, dark dread as a huge, scaled arm reached in through the wall, blotting out the stars.

Rakista had not given them up so easily.

"Look out!" Zilic cried, but far too late.

The beast tore lumps from the walls and the floor, swiping its claws violently left and right. Tiles cracked and glass jars splintered. Shredded paper swept around the chamber like a flock of startled birds, scrawled in the ink of age-old knowledge.

Theodore staggered to a corner and curled up into a tight ball, clasping his hands over his face. The Guardian was not so swift. He watched on in horror between his trembling fingers as a bony knuckle sent the Guardian clattering against the wall and on to the floor in a crumpled heap.

"Come away," Zilic shouted, dragging the boy by an arm.

The Guardian rose to his knees, only for Rakista's claw to send him hurtling through the opening and down to the churning waves below.

Theodore stood dumbstruck, with his eyes gradually turning back to blue. *It's another dream, it has to be!* But this was no dream. It was all too real. A living nightmare. The Guardian had vanished, and with him, every shred of hope.

"Go!" Zilic cried.

There was nothing he could do but run. Theodore darted from the room on the heels of the Borini, panting hard, still lightheaded from whatever sorcery the Guardian had cast upon him.

They took the stairs two at a time to escape, moments before a gigantic plume of sand and dust exploded into the air and the entire tip of the plateau collapsed behind them, sliding down to the ocean in an avalanche of shattered stone slabs and rubble, sending a wave of black saltwater surging away across the surface.

Theodore's ears rang and his breath came ragged. He lay beside Zilic in the grass, too stunned to move. *The Guardian... the Zeon Stones.* His mind raced. "He told me," he whispered to himself. "I know where to find the first one."

Part 2 • Chapter 5

For peace and desire

Clouds drifted through the early morning sky, shimmering white and pink and gold in the light of a new day. The night had crept by, with the companions sheltering from the wind behind the remains of a low stone wall further back along the plateau.

"His name was Legion." Theodore's voice quivered with emotion beneath his hood, traumatised by the incident inside the Guardian's chamber. He held out his hands to animate the staff being laid over them. "One second he was there, then the next..."

Minnie reached for her brother's arm. "It's so awful. What a *horrid* creature. I hope the rocks squashed it flat."

"I can find no trace of the beast," said Olenious from the edge of the plateau. "Once the tide recedes, we shall know for sure." A dozen freckled gulls gathered nearby, ready to polish off any crumbs the visitors might discard.

"Rakista will have to wait," said Zilic. "What else did Legion tell you about the stones?"

"They're called Zeon Stones." Theodore pushed back his hood. "He said the Guardians hid them away years ago, and the dagger, too. But I only learned about one stone. Without him... without Legion, how will we ever find the other two?"

"One stone at a time, Master Reed," said Olenious. "Did you learn of its location?"

Theodore thought for a moment. "A place called the Last Sanctum. Wherever that is."

"The Last Sanctum?" Zilic repeated the name to himself, hoping a memory would spark in his mind. None did.

They sat in silence for a while, listening to the waves crash on to the sand down below and the breeze whistle by. Olenious spoke first. "I may know of this place."

"Really? Is it close by?" Minnie asked excitedly.

"Unfortunately not, Princess." He gestured to the barren landscape away to the west, a vast region of dusty white clay and high stone ridges, stretching for miles. "If I am correct, the place we seek is at the far edge of these lands."

"Beyond the Jurkoon Desert," Zilic muttered, eyeing

the horizon with displeasure.

"There are stories of a shrine hidden within the Moritano Mountains," Olenious continued, tightening his eyepatch. "Their peaks extend along the western edge of the desert sands, stretching as far north as the Giants' Wood. In another tongue, I once heard the shrine referred to as 'Sanctoriun.'"

"Could it be the same place?" Theodore asked. He nibbled at a salted cracker and a gull moved closer in anticipation.

Zilic rubbed his head. "Possibly. I can make little sense of this. Why now? If Legion went to such pains to conceal the dagger and the stones, why reveal them now, after so many years?"

Theodore looked to the floor, slowly recounting the Guardian's words. "He said that Karadas must live in peace... about a poison spreading over the land."

"The Vorath," Olenious growled. "They are a vile curse on the entire realm. Perhaps the enemy were close to finding the weapon? Perhaps that is why it has surfaced only now."

"That would make sense," said Zilic. "If the enemy were to possess the Dagger of Shard, and locate the Zeon Stones... well, that would be a dark day indeed."

Theodore nodded. "Legion said that together, the dagger and the stones can be used to protect the realm. Somehow. Only then can I fulfil my desire," he finished in a mumble.

"And what is your desire, my friend?" Olenious asked.

"To go home," brother and sister answered together. The gulls scattered as Eden swooped down to join Minnie.

Zilic turned to face the Jurkoon Desert again, deep in thought. "Time will be against us, and I fear we shall not be alone in our search for the Zeon Stones."

"So we're going to try and find them?" Theodore asked.

"We are indeed. Peace *must* triumph. Rybas-Kain is already aware of the dagger. If Karadas falls into ruin, our way of life will come to a swift end." Zilic took a knee beside the children. "I promise to see this task through, my friends, to see you home." Neup clicked his jaws, most likely in agreement.

"Alas, I cannot travel with you," said Olenious. "I must return to Galenta, to report to our Queen. Her Highness shall be informed of the developments here."

"Must you go?" The corners of Minnie's mouth sank. She felt far safer with two warriors by her side, even ones as small as the Borini.

"I am a Royal Guard, Princess. I must follow my Queen's commands."

Minnie nodded, smiling to mask her disappointment. Her dimpled cheeks feigned a cheerfulness.

"If you are to travel into the desert, you must all take great care. It is not a place to be underestimated." Olenious rummaged through his backpack for a thick woollen blanket and two unopened food parcels, even offering up his own waterskin. "Please, take these. It will be cold at night. Food and water shall be scarce."

"Thank you, Uncle," said Zilic. He added the provisions to those already strapped to Neup's saddle. "At Galenta, seek Rhal. His studies may have uncovered the location of the other two Zeon Stones. I bid you farewell, Uncle. We are most grateful for your assistance."

"Keep my new friends safe from danger, Zilicarillion. I shall return to you if our Queen permits. I wish you good fortune in this quest." With that, Olenious bowed low, gathered up his pack, and headed back up towards the foothills.

"We depart within the hour," said Zilic, once his uncle had withdrawn. "Rest here. I shall be back shortly."

"Where are you going?" asked Minnie.

"To the jungle, to forage. We shall need as much food as we can carry. Every mouthful will be precious."

The children remained on the plateau with Eden and Neup. Their view from the summit was breath-taking. The impassable ocean stretched before them, with the vibrant jungle and golden sands of Solar Beach running the length of a stunning coastline to the east. But it was to the west they would travel, into a wasteland of dust and stone, and to the desert sands beyond, rising and falling in mercurial patterns all the way to the horizon.

Zilic soon returned with his haul, and the friends

descended the west edge of the plateau. A salty breeze swept past as they clambered down narrow crags beaded with morning dew and crooked ledges worn over time. Step by careful step, they eventually reached the sand on the far side.

The crashing ocean waves were no more than a whisper on the wind by midday, the plateau lost from sight. Zilic and Neup led the way under an increasingly fierce sun through a maze of spiny shrubs and along crumbling ridges pitted with dark holes. This was a barren world moulded from heat and suffering. To heighten their misery, swarms of tedious gnats refused to give them a moment's peace. Even with their cloaks wrapped tightly, the trio were soon covered with itchy red bites.

They spoke little on the way. Theodore and Minnie followed close behind, hurrying around precarious stone towers that cast hardly a shadow and over scorched clay flats, riddled with cracks wide enough to lay train tracks in. Both felt fearful and tired, but the youngsters would find little contentment here. A worn hollow served as a shelter for a few hours when the heat of the afternoon became overwhelming. Only when the temperature subsided did they continue.

"Eden!" Minnie called out as her feathered companion appeared in the sky. The hawk swooped from side to side, seeking a safe route across the terrain, squawking out a warning if one direction or another appeared too precarious. Clay and stone steadily gave way to mile upon mile of hypnotic sand, peppered with tufts of razor-sharp grass. The Jurkoon Desert.

"That is quite far enough for one day," said Zilic as dusk descended over the land. The setting sun touched the western horizon to cast a vivid pink-ruby glow across the sky. "We shall enter the dunes at first light."

Both Theodore and his sister were more than pleased to stop.

They rested for the night beside a rare spring burbling amongst a cluster of rocks as white as a swan's feathers. Tall dry grass and a small fruit tree grew close by, clinging to life in the wilderness.

"Have you ever crossed this land, Zilic?" asked Theodore. He topped up the water skins from the spring while Minnie plucked lilac berries from the tree.

Zilic shook his head. He gazed thoughtfully towards the dunes, gathering dried grass and twigs for a fire. "I go with you by choice. But I must confess, I am deeply troubled by the Jurkoon Desert."

The siblings shared an uneasy glance. Neither relished the prospect of heading out on to the sand. With their Borini guide openly expressing his concern, they were now even less enthusiastic. Still, after a bland meal of crackers and berries, the children slept, lulled into a slumber by the murmur of trickling water.

***

At dawn, Theodore and Minnie drank deeply from the spring and fastened their boots tight. They entered the desert beside Neup, heading around the first of a thousand sculpted dunes stretching as far as their eyes could see. Ripples of heat danced on the surface under a wide clear sky, where not even the merest hint of a cloud could be seen. Eden's white wings were the only blemish on the bright blue canvas.

Mile upon mile of monotonous, strength-sapping sand passed by, with only an occasional hunk of worn rock or tuft of parched grass to break the mundane scenery. After half a day of continual misery, the children more than felt the strain, shuffling forward at an ever-slowing pace with their shoulders slumped forward. Both had already grown weary of the Jurkoon Desert.

"It *must* end soon?" Minnie groaned. "I've never been so hot." *Never, ever.*

"We have barely begun," said Zilic. His hairless head glistened with sweat beads. "The Moritano Mountains are still many miles from here."

Minnie huffed. "I hope Olenious was right about this sanctum place. It might not even exist after all this!"

"My uncle's knowledge of the realm is renowned among our people. We must trust in his judgement."

"Why do you think it's called the Last Sanctum?"

asked Theodore, stumbling over his own boots for the umpteenth time.

"That, Master Reed, we shall have to discover together."

"I imagine it'll be well hidden, won't it?" *Concealed, and possibly well-guarded,* he thought fretfully.

"Indeed. We are in agreement on that point, my friend."

The afternoon's heat forced their journey to a halt once again, but there were no hollows to shelter in out here. Instead, they used the wooden poles and a canvas sheet that Neup had carried to erect a cramped sunshade. The children were soon resting in its shadow, snacking on cubes of melon and orange segments wrapped in mint leaves. They gazed out over the hazy landscape as they ate, breathing in a curiously sweet aroma wafting on the air. There were no signs of life to be seen, only sand and silence. At the very least, the gnats were no longer around to pester them.

Once the call came to move on, Minnie and Theodore grudgingly dismantled their canopy and followed Zilic up the slope of the next dune in their path, a dune indistinguishable from those already trodden. Through late afternoon and into early evening, the companions struggled up and down and around a hundred more, on and on into the golden sea.

"It'll get dark soon, Zilic." Theodore held up a hand to shield his eyes from the sun. "What do we do then?"

Zilic paused to let the boy catch up. "By day, these

sands are perilous. By night, well, it would be most unwise to travel by night. We must find a place to shelter."

"Shelter... out here?" Minnie looked around. "It's just sand. Endless sand."

On and on they struggled, with their strength and spirits waning with each tired step. Darkness would come soon; a chill had already arrived. The sun quivered on the horizon, and an eerie red glow spread across the sky.

While their canvas sheet made for a sufficient sunshade, night-time in the desert called for a more substantial refuge, if such a place existed here. Zilic went on ahead to search further afield, leaving the siblings with only Neup's claw prints as a guide.

The children felt decidedly uneasy. Zilic had yet to return, and the surrounding desert grew darker by the minute. Eden took to the sky, but returned with no encouragement.

"They'll be back soon," said Theodore. He sifted through his arrows and fiddled with his bow to shield his own anxiety. *Come back, Zilic,* he pleaded. *Where are you? You have to come back!*

Neither heard the Terap approach. Neup scuttled up the dune behind them at speed and came to a skidding halt. "Come now," Zilic called in a low voice, wheeling Neup around. "You must hurry."

Theodore threw back his hood. "Zilic... you made us jump!"

"My apologies, Master Reed. Please, you must both follow me."

"Did you find a place to shelter?" asked Minnie.

Zilic nodded. His emerald eyes were wide and alive, scanning the dunes; his face flushed with concern. "Not far from here. My friends, you must come *now.* I fear we are not alone out here."

Part 2 • Chapter 6

Fire and anguish

"What was it, Zilic? What did you see?" Theodore's face had turned ash white.

Minnie drove the point of her bow into the sand to stop herself from sliding down the smooth face of a sweeping dune. "Please, Theo. Hurry up!"

Zilic led the children across the cooling sand to a shallow, gravelly bowl, where a dozen spindly cacti thrust up from the ground to cast long, dark shadows. A tight outcrop of smooth, yellowed stones in their midst made for a most welcome sight. In their current plight, the stones looked as comfortable as any palace, an ideal sanctuary to see out the night.

Neither hesitated. Theodore and Minnie dashed forward to squeeze inside, slumping down against the still-warm boulders. Neup scuttled up and over the top instead, scraping against the stones with six clawed feet.

"What did you see?" Theodore asked again. *What has him so spooked?*

Zilic paused before joining the others. He peered out into the growing gloom, flexing the string of his bow. "My eyes saw nothing, Master Reed. It was a noise, a curious rattle. Neup heard it, too."

Neup clicked.

"A rattle... what sort of rattle?" Minnie whispered. *That doesn't sound good.*

Zilic knelt before the children and leant his bow up against the rocks. "A rather unfriendly rattle. Something is out there on the sand, an animal of great size, I fear. A substantial threat."

Theodore swallowed his fear, but immediately it returned. "But I've not seen anything alive out here, not even a fly!"

"The desert is a barren, harsh land," said Zilic. "But there are creatures that endure here. They appear mostly at night... mostly," he added ominously.

As the children reflected on the Borini's discouraging words, twilight faded from the world, smothered by the darkness of the night. A flutter in the air momentarily startled the friends, but it was only Eden. She swooped down to settle on Neup's saddle, tilting her head to gaze down at the companions huddled among the rocks.

"She didn't cry out," said Minnie. "Eden didn't squawk or screech. If danger was close by, she would have let us know."

"She's right," Theodore agreed, more in hope than certainty.

"An encouraging sign," Zilic muttered. He turned to look out into the blackness. "We must remain vigilant through the night. A fire cannot be risked, nor a lantern. We must be invisible."

Minnie and Theodore nodded. They felt more than happy to follow the Borini's advice, despite the plummeting temperature and whatever it was lurking close by. All heat from the ground and the air vanished within the hour, replaced by a bitter chill to turn their breath into mist. Even pressed together under their cloaks and blankets, the children shivered.

A sky of countless silver stars made for a magnificent night-time display, but it was a view that none of them could fully enjoy. The siblings nibbled at flat breads with chattering teeth and a few of the berries Minnie had gathered.

It took some time, but sleep came to them eventually, an uncomfortable sleep tormented by dreams of endless sand and sinister rattles. Zilic remained alert throughout the night, eyeing the sand for any hint of a threat.

***

They awoke early the next morning to a wonderful smell. Zilic knelt in the shade beside a small cook fire, turning strips of meat on wooden sticks above the flames. "Good morning, my friends," he said in a cheerful tone. "The night, I am pleased to report, passed without a disturbance."

Theodore brushed the sleep dust from his eyes and scratched at a maddening bite on his neck. "Do you think it will come back?"

"While the heat of the day remains, I think not. Neup and I searched the area at first light. The sands are quiet."

"How far are the mountains from here?" Theodore climbed up on to a rock, keen to see an end to the dunes and catch a glimpse of the Moritano Mountains. *Nothing but sand,* he thought sourly, gazing all around. *Sand, sand, and yet more sand.*

"Not far, Master Reed." In truth, Zilic had no way of knowing for sure.

"This is delicious. Come and try some, Theo." Minnie felt far safer in the light of the new day. "Where did you find it?"

Zilic pointed to a set of tiny tracks in the sand. "You have our feathered friend to thank; Eden, as you have named her. She moved as quick as an arrow to snare your morning meal."

"Where is she now?"

"Off hunting for a meal of her own, I suspect," said Zilic, turning the sticks.

The day had barely begun and already it felt scorching hot. While Minnie emptied the sand from her boots, her brother leant against the rocks and drew the crystal dagger from his pack. He slowly caressed the frosted blade, pondering its role in all of this. *The Dagger of Shard. How can this thing possibly get us all the way home?* As he sat with his thoughts, a silent shadow passed across the sun to briefly blot out the light.

Neup clicked nervously and Zilic leapt to his feet in a flash, scooping sand over the glowing coals. He looking to the sky with wide, anxious eyes, twisting his head left and right, fearful of what they might see.

"What is it?" asked Minnie. She could sense his concern.

Finally, the Borini spied it; a crimson wyvern, soaring through the air on broad tattered wings. "Hide!" he cried, urging Minnie between the rocks. "It's him! Rybas-Kain, he hunts for us."

Theodore's heart thumped inside his chest. Dark memories came flooding back of the day he had faced the giant warrior below the Aradine Mountains, an event he never wished to experience again.

The children cowered between the rocks beside Neup as the shadow passed over again. A piercing screech and the whip of leathery wings tortured their ears. Minnie glimpsed the beast through a gap in the stones and panic gripped her stomach tight. But as swiftly as the monster and its master had appeared, they departed, cutting through the warm air with menace, drifting away to the east.

Theodore crept out on to the sand once his body had stopped trembling. The desert remained still, eerily silent, with wisps of white dust twirling over the surface. "If Rybas-Kain comes back... and we're out in the open..."

"Indeed," said Zilic. "We go, now. We must get out of this desert with all haste." The Borini vaulted up to Neup's back as the children gathered their belongings.

They watched the sky for what felt like an eternity before hurrying over the baking sand at a fast pace, keeping to the dips between the dunes to stay out of sight. All three expected to hear the whoosh of wyvern wings again at any moment.

"It's the Dagger of Shard he wants," Theodore panted. "So long as I have it, we'll never be safe." *I wish it had never come to me.*

Zilic shook his head, peering up and all around. "While you possess the weapon, Master Reed, the future of the realm remains safe. I, for one, intend to keep it that way."

Hours passed without rest. Their legs were sore and their necks ached from looking skywards. The unseen creature from the previous day, with its menacing rattle, that was now almost forgotten, a lesser terror.

Minnie prayed they would discover another cluster of rocks to hide amongst, but by midday, around each and every sand mound they passed, she had found little more than a pebble.

For the first time since entering the desert, the weather changed. A steady breeze whipped across the surface and soft, pale clouds drifted past the sun to bring some relief to their skin, if only for a few delightful seconds.

"A storm's brewing," said Zilic, sniffing at the air. "We are too exposed. We must find another place to shelter. I shall scout ahead. I can travel faster alone."

"We can't split up now!" Minnie cried. "He'll find us. I *know* he will."

Zilic jumped down to stand before the children. "I think not. The creature Rybas-Kain rides upon, the wyvern, it cannot fly in a sand storm. We, on the other hand, we shall be buried from our heads to our boots if we do not take action."

Minnie rubbed at her dry lips, looking to her brother for reassurance.

Theodore remained silent. *I don't like this either,* he thought.

"Wait for me here." Zilic checked his bow and settled back into his saddle. "I shall return before sunset." With that, he and Neup disappeared into the swirl and bluster of the growing sand storm.

Eden returned soon after, unable to stay airborne. She

perched on Minnie's quiver and dipped her head under a ruffled wing. The children sat in wait as instructed, bundled up in their cloaks, gradually blending into the desert as it gathered around their legs and at their back. Sand lashed their bodies, and the wind screamed past their ears.

"Where are they, Theo?"

"What?"

Minnie moved closer to be heard above the gale. "Where are they?"

"I don't know," he yelled back. "They should be back by now. We *can't* stay here."

"You want to stay here?"

"I said... we have to move; the sand will bury us alive. Come on, we need to go. We have no choice." *Where are you, Zilic?*

Minnie nodded an agreement through a chink in her hood.

The sun could barely be seen through the chaos. It could well have been night-time for all they knew. They struggled on regardless at a pace barely more than a shuffle. Neither had any confidence the sand storm would ever end.

A fierce blast of wind forced Theodore to his knees at the peak of a sharp ridge, whipping the hood back over his head and filling his eyes and mouth with sand. His vision faded to a painful haze. "Minnie," he screamed. He spun in circles, trying to face in every direction at once. "Minnie? Minnie, where are you?"

Sand and wind battered him from all sides, but no matter which way he faced or however loud he called out, his sister would not appear. She had vanished completely. Theodore staggered around blindly, hopelessly lost on the windswept dunes, with his tears turning to a sludgy paste around his eyes. He screamed until his throat felt raw. "Minnie! Come back. Where are you?" *Not again. I can't lose you again.*

A deep sense of dread pulsed inside his chest, driving his mind to distraction. He imagined every dark blur to be the silhouette of Rybas-Kain approaching with his battle-axe raised high. Each wail of the wind became the phantom roar of a wyvern and a whoosh of ragged wings.

The ground fell away to put an end to his torment, dragging him down to the surface and burying him to the chest, with his voice calling out meekly into his swirling, sandy nightmare.

Part 2 • Chapter 7

Dance of delight

Minnie had not laid eyes on her brother for half a day now. *Where are you, Theo?* Her night alone in the desert had been a terrifying experience, with only a cloak to protect her from the elements. Every minute felt like an hour; every hour she imagined would be her last in life.

At the first glimmer of sunrise, Minnie had wept openly, and although the day brought an unbearable heat, it was far preferable to the black chill of the night. It took the warmth of the morning sun over an hour to thaw her out fully.

A moderate breeze remained from the sand storm as

she trudged the newly sculpted desert, adjusting her bow and quiver, steadily cooking in the fearsome temperature. Her mouth felt as dry as the surrounding desert. In every direction, fresh sand stretched away to the horizon. All footprints and tracks from the previous day had simply blown away, erased for all time.

Eden circled overhead, squawking excitedly. She landed close by, flapping her wings before launching back up to the sky.

"What is it, girl? Is it Theo? Have you seen him?"

The thought filled her with fresh hope. Minnie made her way around a colossal dune and up yet another steep bank, but it wasn't long before the hawk had disappeared from sight, her snowy feathers lost against the wispy patchwork of cloud high above. "Come back Eden."

She kept a watchful eye out for the wyvern, too, and the master on its back. The chances of escaping Rybas-Kain would be slim to none if he should appear, alone as she was.

Minnie had almost given up any hope of ever finding her brother. She huffed and halted at the rim of a sweeping sand ridge, holding up an arm to shield the sun from her eyes. A long-eared rabbit scampered past to startle her, and then another, faster than the first. They vanished over the next dune in a spiral of dust. Both seemed in a desperate hurry.

All the colour drained from her face as a dull rattle

echoed over the sand. *The creature... the rattle!* Minnie shrank down and flattened her body against the ridge, horror-struck by what her eyes had just seen. An enormous blood red scorpion stalked across the surface on eight spindly legs, nipping at the air with pincers the size of tombstones. "Don't come this way," she begged, but her pleas went unanswered.

The scorpion turned to head in her direction, halting an arm's length above her head. A needle-sharp stinger glistened in the sunlight, sleek and deadly at the tip of a segmented tail arced over its armoured body.

Minnie shuffled lower, using her hands and feet, feeling the warm sand trickle down her neck. Every vein pulsed. *No, no, no, it can't be,* her thoughts whispered. *Zilic, you said they only came at night-time.* She didn't dare to breathe as a bristled leg landed beside her shoulder, creaking as it settled. Her eyes snapped shut and her entire body felt paralysed.

Sand washed over her as the scorpion scuttled down the ridge at speed, hissing and rattling its tail, keen to hunt down a fluffle of wide-eyed rabbits bounding across the sand.

She didn't hesitate, not for a second. Minnie raced away, breathing hard, not daring to look back. Sweat and dust stung her eyes and her bow and quiver smacked painfully against her head and hips, but she would not stop. "Stay away... stay away from me."

Eventually, exhaustion set in and her legs gave way at the peak of the latest sand mound of that day. Minnie scrambled over the top to look down upon a magical sight. *Trees... out here?* she thought.

It took a moment for her eyes to adjust to the vibrant array of lemon and lime leaves, and plants painted in a hundred different shades of green. She brushed the red hair from her face to gaze down a long, gradual slope, to where an island of palm trees and vegetation grew at the centre of a wide sandy basin. "It's a forest among the dunes," she whispered, unsure if the vision was genuine, or merely a spiteful mirage conjured up by the desert.

Either way, with the scorpion close by, she dared not linger. Minnie charged down the slope and into the jungle, elbowing her way through the vines and dense, stiff leaves flecked with dried sap. The foliage brought an instant relief from the searing heat.

Thoughts tormented her mind, visions of pincers snapping at her limbs, and the petrified rabbits darting away to safety. *Poor little things.* She thought about her brother, too, but also about water. Her waterskin had been lost in the night and her lips now ached for the cool touch of water. Even a sip from a muddy puddle would be a blessing.

Minnie pushed past jade and burgundy shrubs twice her own height, breathing in the humid air and calling out to her brother. "Theo. Theo, are you here?" Dead leaves and branches crunched under her boots. The undergrowth eventually opened out to reveal an exquisite garden of unrivalled beauty, shaded by a canopy of crimped palm leaves. *This is so beautiful.* Flowers grew all around, some in colours she never knew existed. Delicate seed pods wrapped in feathery bundles floated through the air on a gentle breeze over a mossy lawn, where a narrow crystal-clear lake stretched away under the trees. *It's a paradise.*

"Theo, Zilic... are you here?"

Tiny birds with lilac feathers and butterflies as large as her hands darted from flower to flower, gathering pollen and paying little attention to the strange young girl.

"Zilic, can you hear me?"

When no reply came back, Minnie crouched beside the pool to dip her weathered hands into the water, sending ripples dancing away over the surface. Relief and delight raced through her body as she took a deep drink. A touch of energy returned, with the hypnotic, sweet scent in the air helping to rejuvenate her further.

She removed her boots and weaved between the ferns and flowers, allowing the moss to caress her sandy toes. The sight of a domed hut set back in the shadows brought her to a standstill. "Hello. Is anyone there?" She could see two other huts under the trees, crafted from timber and baked mud, with their pasty yellow roofs splattered with resin. The settlement appeared abandoned at first glance, but on closer inspection, her eyes noticed fresh fish skewered by wooden stakes and a spread of coals glowing in a primitive brick stove.

Minnie screamed and jumped back as her brother burst through the shrubs at her side. Birds and butterflies scattered as Eden swooped down into the clearing, followed closely by Neup and Zilic.

"Theo, you're here." She threw herself into his arms and held him tight, feeling delight, relief, and confusion all at the same moment.

"We searched *everywhere* for you," Theodore insisted. "Where did you go?"

Minnie wiped away a tear and hugged him again. "One minute you were in front of me, the next, well... I couldn't see a thing. Then that creature came after me, the rattly one. It was *huge*, Theo, huge!"

"I must apologise," said Zilic. He looked at the floor, his face furrowed with regret. "It was a mistake to leave you both. I must ask for forgiveness."

"You don't have anything to forgive, silly." Minnie knelt to hug the Borini. "You're the bravest person I know."

Theodore tugged lightly at her hair and cleared his throat. "I thought you said *I* was the bravest person you knew?" Laughter filled the garden and genuine dimples formed in his sister's cheeks, overjoyed that the Jurkoon Desert had failed to get the better of them—so far.

"From now on, can we all just stay together and..."

Before Minnie could finish speaking, a band of slight figures appeared across the lawn, planting their sharp spears into the moss. The tallest looked to be four feet at most. Every one wore a mask made from bark and decorative beads. Every one looked a threat.

"It's all right," said Theodore, noting his sister's dismay. "They're friends. They won't harm us."

Minnie chewed her thumbnail, unconvinced.

"This is Dita," said Zilic, gesturing to the smallest member of the group. "He is the chief of the Taanu clan. They are distant relatives of the Borini, in fact. The Taanu have welcomed us into their home."

Dita stepped forward, removed his mask and signalled for his tribe to do likewise. In total, twelve Taanu had gathered. All were male, with dark bronze skin and cropped, frizzy white hair. Their eyes were wide and green, though not as vivid and full of life as their Borini relations. Loincloths hung down at their waists, decorated with petals, and coloured beads hung from their ears, stretched low by the weight.

They do look quite like the Borini, Minnie thought. *But old, so very old.*

"The Taanu fled their home many years ago," Zilic went on, "driven into the desert by the Vorath. By some miracle, they stumbled upon this oasis. They call it Valmire. It translates as 'safe place' in their tongue." Dita's eyes held a deep sorrow as Zilic finished the story. "Only a handful of the Taanu endured. Many were hunted, though most perished in the fiery hell of the Jurkoon Desert."

Even now, over a century on, Dita could not celebrate their survival fully.

"They saved me, Minnie. I was half-buried, so terrified I'd lost you again. Then they found me."

Dita smiled and the wrinkled skin around his cheeks smoothed. He clapped twice and motioned to his tribe with a mixture of hand signals and high-pitched whistles. Immediately, the Taanu busied themselves around the village.

"There is to be a feast tonight in Valmire," Zilic announced. "Dita has declared us his guests of honour."

Minnie and Theodore hugged once again, relieved to be back together, ignoring the sad truth that they would soon have to go back out on to the sand. At that moment, both would happily have stayed within the tranquil surrounds of Valmire forever. They strolled around the garden, chatting and laughing and kneeling to sample each distinct scent of the many-coloured flowers.

Eden watched on from a domed roof as twilight drew in, with her eager black eyes set firmly on a pile of fish being readied for the cook pot. Rhythmic drums echoed over the water and out through the trees as the tribe hung tiny orange lanterns from the branches, each one flickering like a joyful firefly.

The Taanu and their guests enjoyed a meagre feast

that evening under a sky of countless stars. They ate rock hard blocks of bread, but most of the food on offer was fish, netted from the pool at the centre of the garden. There were black fish wrapped in vines, bright green fish pressed in crushed seeds, and coral fish stuffed with wild herbs. Even fish stuffed with other fish. There were eggs, too. Boiled pink eggs. Minnie ate hers without letting Eden see, unsure if the bird would take offence. It had to be said that the food tasted fairly disagreeable, but to Theodore and Minnie, on this night, it was the most welcome meal they had ever eaten.

After supper, the Taanu performed an unusual dance on the lawn, leaping and twirling to the restful music drifting around the garden and out on to the cooling sands. The siblings sat close by, giggling at the show.

"No, no," Minnie squealed. Her grin faded as the Taanu dragged her and her brother up to join in with the dancing. They moved as freely as the Taanu once they were relaxed. Neither could quite recall the last time they had laughed and larked with such merriment.

Dita and Zilic moved away to talk beside a clay brazier, using symbols and gestures to fill the many gaps in their varied speech. Zilic spoke at length about Borini and their fine city, Galenta, while Dita recounted in more detail how his own people had discovered Valmire, out in the Jurkoon Desert. When the conversation turned back to Zilic, and to why he and the youngsters risked their lives to cross the dunes, Dita's eyes filled with intrigue.

"Friends, come and sit with us," Zilic called over to the children. "Our host has important knowledge that may interest us."

The siblings sat cross-legged to hear Dita speak unknown words in a croaky voice. Zilic did his best to translate. "It seems we are not as far away as I first thought. The Moritano Mountains are a day or so to the west of here. It appears that my uncle was correct. The Last Sanctum *is* located among the mountain peaks."

"Sanctoriun," said Dita. He wiggled his fingers to depict falling water and held up three spindly fingers on his other hand, mumbling all the while.

Again, Zilic translated. "Three waterfalls—the sanctum we seek is within a narrow ravine into which these three falls merge."

"Waterfalls?" said Minnie, more confused than ever.

"They conceal the entrance," Zilic explained. "We shall find the doorway at the base of the ravine, carved through the rock."

"But how does he know all of this?" asked Theodore, staring at Dita.

Zilic listened again before answering. His expression held misgiving. "Several years ago, the Taanu travelled to the Moritano Mountains. Six journeyed to the peaks in search of food and perhaps a more fitting location to settle, though only one of their party returned."

"What did they find?" the children asked together.

"The Last Sanctum, shrouded in a veil of mist. But an uneasiness, a darkness lurked inside. The Taanu did not linger and made their way back to Valmire."

Minnie remained confused. "But you said only one of them came home?"

"Indeed," said Zilic. "Only Dita himself made it back here alive. Between here and the mountains, beyond even the desert, there is a wasteland where the clay underfoot is stained red. The Jetta Deep."

"Red?" asked Theodore. "Stained red from what?"

"It is not the colour of the ground that should concern us, Master Reed, but what lies beneath. We must take great care. Below the Jetta Deep live the Massuki, 'serpents of the underworld,' if my interpretation is correct."

The conversation fell silent, and the dancing had ended. Even with sunburnt skin, the siblings grew peaky, and their stomachs sank deep into their feet. They gazed into the brazier as a sad flute ballad played softly nearby. After hearing Dita's warning, Valmire no longer held the same ambience as it had done only a short while ago.

"This gets worse and worse," Minnie grumbled, massaging her ear lobes. "So, before we even get to search for this haunted sanctum, we have to walk across miles and miles of red land with giant snakes underneath ready to gobble us up? And that horrid thing with the pincers... that's still out there too!" With that, she trudged away to sit alone beside the water.

You forgot Rybas-Kain, Theodore almost blurted, but thought better of it. No one needed a reminder of the full list of dangers they faced; a list growing longer with each new day.

Zilic forced a smile and leant in to speak quietly to the boy. "There is a small amount of good news, Master Reed. The Guardian's memories are accurate. The Zeon Stone we seek is located at the Last Sanctum. Dita looked upon it with his very own eyes."

"Really?" Theodore's mood brightened and his confidence grew. "If Dita made it across the Jetta Deep, then surely we can, too. We have to." *It's the only hope we have.*

"I believe so, too, my friend," Zilic agreed, this time with a genuine smile. "I believe so, too."

Part 2 • Chapter 8

The red waste

They set out from Valmire as dawn broke, with a caution that fresh sand storms seemed likely that day. The oasis soon lay far behind, hidden again among the sea of endless dunes.

Dita had offered four of his tribesmen as a parting gift. They walked in silence a short distance ahead, tasked with guiding Zilic and the children to the fringes of the Jetta Deep, but no further. With only a dozen of his people left in the world, the Taanu could not afford to lose anymore.

It took all of Theodore's persuasive powers to convince his sister they would be safe along the way, while remaining quite unconvinced himself.

"What if that creature comes back?" asked Minnie. Every fibre of her body yearned for home, to return to the farm in England where she and her brother had grown up. She wanted it so much it hurt. Minnie knew in her heart that the Zeon Stones were the key to that ever happening—a prize surely worth risking their lives for. Eventually, she agreed, and soon all thoughts turned to the path ahead.

The procession marched under a clear blue sky for almost an entire day. Eden soared on a light breeze overhead to keep watch over the travellers. Gradually, the shade and firmness of the surface altered from light golden sand to burnt orange clay, interwoven with thick twists of crimson shingle.

"We are approaching the Jetta Deep," Zilic announced.

"Are they the Moritano Mountains?" Theodore peered into the distance, over a bleak landscape of baked red clay where spindly thistles poked up between countless cracks in the ground, reaching up for a drop of rain that may never fall.

"They are indeed," said Zilic. "I must say, they do not compare favourably with the mountains of Aradine. Although I am rather biased." The Borini spoke the truth. The slate mountains to the west were nothing like the sculpted peaks rising above Galenta. Instead, the Moritano Mountains appeared as a vast pile of crumbled grey-black rock, barren and unwelcoming.

Theodore nodded in agreement and rubbed his elbows,

hardly relishing the prospect of venturing there.

It was here that the Taanu held up their spears in a farewell gesture. Without a word, all four turned around and began their long trek back to Valmire. Minnie stood solemnly, waving until they were out of sight. She wished they could have travelled on, maybe just a little further. "I didn't get to say thank you," she mumbled sadly. *I wonder what the Taanu word for thank you is?*

The remaining companions set up a modest camp beside a low sandbank as dusk loomed. Theodore and Minnie soon had a warm fire burning, using dried thistles for kindling and chopped wood from their provisions. Next, they prepared their meal. It would be fish once again. The Taanu had kindly provided an ample supply before leaving Valmire. With little food for their own tribe, it was a truly generous gift.

Neup kept watch above the sandbank while Zilic ventured out on to the red clay, pressing a tiny ear to the ground, listening for any hint of movement. Darkness had drawn in by the time he returned. The Borini set down his pack and bow, patted Neup's glossy shell and joined the siblings by the fire.

"What did you hear?" asked Theodore, tearing at a chunk of blackened bread.

"Nothing, thankfully. If the sands are quiet, the Massuki should be far away. I shall check again before we attempt our crossing."

Minnie frowned. "How do you know what they sound like?"

"And what if they lay still?" Theodore added. "Do they make a noise if they don't move?"

"Try not to worry about such things. Get some sleep. I shall watch over the camp tonight." In truth, he had no answers to their questions.

The siblings sat in silence under a blanket. Both felt uneasy about the following day. If luck was with them, they would pass over the red waste unnoticed and unharmed. Neither dared to think of the alternative.

***

It was still dark when Zilic roused them from sleep. "We go now," he whispered from the shadow of his grey hood.

The children gathered their belongings without hesitation and walked tiredly over to where Neup waited. Eden fluttered overhead, with her feathers shining like brushed silver in the moonlight.

"I hear nothing but silence," Zilic said in a low voice. "We must take this opportunity. Step delicately," he added. "Any vibration or noise could alert the Massuki to our presence."

They set out in single file, creeping forward one soft step at a time. It was slow but steady progress. The sky had turned a pale purple by the time the sun appeared on the eastern horizon behind them. Bone dry clay crunched underfoot as they walked beside the bank of a shallow riverbed that hadn't felt a trickle of water in a year or more. Partially collapsed burrows vanished underground, and silvery spiral shells and ashen driftwood lay here and there among the furrows.

"Maybe the Massuki things are all dead," Minnie muttered to herself, relaxing a touch. "They must be. There's nothing to eat here." *I hope they all died.* Eden swooped down to rest her wings before letting out a piercing shriek.

The hawk wheeled away to hover close by and Neup tilted up in a defensive pose, stretching his jaws wide.

"Don't move!" said Zilic.

Minnie froze. She sensed a movement at her back and heard the grind of clay and sand steadily shifting. *Theo, help me,* she begged silently, too afraid to turn and look herself. Frightful images flashed through her mind, of monsters and demons that even a nightmare would be fearful to conjure.

The dread in her brother's eyes told her she was in grave danger. Theodore stood with his hands clenched, wishing he could help, but terrified to help. He watched in awe as a powerful serpentine body emerged from the ground behind his sister. The Massuki looked to be at least sixty feet in length. Stiff barbs quivered along its sleek black flanks and a smooth pointed skull shimmered in the sunlight, angled perfectly to burrow beneath the earth. The smell was nearly as appalling as its appearance, a nasty blend of rotting meat and filthy sewer water.

"Why doesn't it attack?" Theodore whispered.

"If we make no movement, the Massuki cannot sense us. They have no sight. They hunt by sound and feel alone."

Oily, red tentacles darted out from under the Massuki's skull, raking over the surface like metallic hooks, as if tasting the clay. Each swish brought them ever closer to the girl's boots.

It took all of Minnie's courage not to flee. If she moved—even slightly—the Massuki would strike, and with nowhere to hide, her end would be swift. "Zilic. Theo," she mouthed. "Help me. Do something!"

But it was their smallest companion who came to her aid. The beast let out a guttural moan and hissed as Eden clawed and nipped at the tentacles with her beak and talons. Attack and retreat. It was a distraction, nothing more.

Zilic scanned the horizon for a sliver of hope; and hope he found. It was a significant risk to be sure, but the Massuki would devour each of them in turn if they hesitated a moment longer. It had to be now.

"Over there. We must run," said Zilic. He pointed to a heap of pale boulders and dead tree trunks in the distance, scattered above a sandbank.

Run? Theodore almost cried out. *He has to be out of his tiny mind!* His heart thumped at the prospect of outrunning the Massuki.

"Toward the mountains. Do not falter. Whatever happens, do not look back." Zilic nocked three arrows to his bow and aimed for the sky. The arrows whistled high into the air, where they seemed to hang forever. A hundred feet to their left, they struck the ground. *Thud, thump, thud.* The Massuki paused with its tentacles quivering, before easing itself back into the earth.

"It's going," Theodore whispered.

Zilic held him back. "Not yet. Wait. Wait."

The monster blew a loud wet snort and tunnelled back into the clay, almost tipping Minnie on to her back in its haste.

"Steady... steady. *Now!* Go, go, run, my friends."

Minnie needed no encouragement. She and Theodore sprinted over the loose clay, desperate to reach the safety of solid stone. They almost toppled to the ground as a livid shriek rang out behind them.

"It's coming back!" Theodore cried out.

The Massuki quickly figured out their ploy and abandoned stealth. It came at speed, surging headlong below the surface to hunt down its deceitful victims.

Neup had already reached the sandbank by the time Zilic and the children arrived. It quickly became clear to their eyes that it was neither rock nor tree trunks up ahead, but the ancient remains of a gigantic, four-legged creature. Thick blanched bones thrust up from the ground beside a half-buried skull, tilted to one side. A massive ten-foot horn jutted out from its brow and a scraggy bird's nest hung down limply from a round eye socket where the giant would once have looked out upon the world.

"Climb up," said Zilic. "There may be more..."

The Massuki ploughed into the skeleton, grinding against the bones to send fragments scattering in all directions, yet it hardly made a dent.

The children clambered up and away from the seething creature. Chips and dints in the weathered bones made the task simple enough, and within a minute they were high up and out of reach of the Massuki. Eden came to rest beside Minnie, preening the feathers dislodged during her heroic act.

"Are you all right, Minnie?" Theodore asked, once his breathing had calmed. "It came out of nowhere." He looked down in dismay to see the clay buckle. The predator circled the bones over and over, scarcely breaking the surface.

"And that smell," said Minnie. "Terrible, like one of Aunt Cordelia's home-cooked meals."

Theodore had to laugh. "Were you not scared?"

"Absolutely terrified! Maybe I'm just getting used to this place. *Everything* here wants to eat me."

"Not everything," Zilic smiled, tapping his smooth head. "You are truly brave. I would not hesitate to enlist you both as Royal Guards. I shall share the tale of your bravery with my Queen on our return."

"Thank you, Zilic," Theodore said proudly. He sat in silence for a while, visualising himself dressed in steel armour with a sword in his hand, ready to head out to battle a host of ghastly monsters.

There was little comfort to be had, and by midday the sun cooked the land below. A kink in the surface drew Minnie's eye as she drank from a waterskin. "Down there. Look, another one."

Theodore's eyes widened. "Zilic, what do we do? There're *two* of them now."

The entire skeleton shook before Zilic could even think to comment. A rank smell came first, followed by the black skull and half-body of a Massuki. Swirling tentacles tugged at the bones, seeking to topple them to the ground.

"Do something," Minnie screamed.

Neup reacted quickly, scuttling down to jab at the beast with his two scythed mandibles, but it was the arrows loosed from the Borini's bow that forced the Massuki back under the surface, groaning, with its hide peppered with arrow shafts. "They'll dig us out from beneath, given the chance," Zilic yelled.

"Then we won't give them that chance," Theodore said defiantly, working clumsily to nock an arrow to his bow.

Minnie followed her brother's lead and aimed a shaky arrow at the ground. The siblings had yet to even try out their new weapons, though both were ready to at least try to defend their position.

They sat in wait for over an hour with their arrows nocked, and bows ready to draw. The heat increased minute by minute to reach an unbearable temperature. Even their silk cloaks—tailored to keep the wearer cool—failed to repel the sun's rays fully. The friends could only sit and suffer, marooned high up, with their supply of water running dangerously low. It was well into the afternoon before a welcome breeze swept past and clouds arrived to dot the open sky.

Theodore picked at the bones with an arrowhead. "I think this might have been an elephant, you know."

Minnie frowned. "An elephant? It's too big to be an elephant," she teased. "And they don't have a horn, silly. They have tusks."

"Well, a giant one, then. And they could have horns for all you know. Here on Karadas, I mean."

Her hazel eyes rolled, and she urged Zilic to agree with her. "Tell him, Zilic, it *can't* be an elephant. Can it?"

"I do not know of this creature you speak of."

Minnie smirked. "See, Theo. I told you."

"These are the remains of a Malla Danto."

"A Malla what?" asked Theodore.

"Malla… Danto," Zilic repeated slowly, rubbing his hand over a flaking rib. "I have never seen a living specimen. Few in the realm have. It is a rare beast indeed."

"I wish the Massuki were rare," said Theodore. "Extinct would be better."

"Have they not gone yet?" Minnie asked.

"I think not." said Zilic. "I imagine the Massuki can wait for days, even weeks, for food. Watch." He hacked at a loose chunk of bone using a silver dagger and tossed it out on to the open ground. Immediately, not one, but four large shapes darted beneath the surface to investigate.

Theodore watched on in dismay. "Four of them?" *How will we ever escape this?* As soon as they set foot on to the sand, the Massuki would hunt them all, no matter which way they ran. Each of them would be dragged down and devoured. *This is hopeless,* he thought gloomily. *Dita was right about this awful place. We should never have come here.*

***

Night-time came and went with no further movement. None of them had slept a wink. All three now despaired at their situation. The Massuki were in no hurry. They would wait patiently for their victims to climb down, or perish from the heat and fall to the ground. Either way, the Massuki would claim their meal.

"If only I knew how to control the blade," Theodore muttered, caressing the Dagger of Shard. "It helped us before, against Rybas-Kain. Why doesn't it help us now?"

"Indeed," Zilic agreed. "It would be of great assistance."

Silence echoed as the sun rose to cast long shadows across the Jetta Deep. The companions shared food and drink around, but few words. The fish tasted of sand, the water too. They had been here too long.

Zilic drew in a deep breath. "I can see only one option. We have to run. We have no other choice."

"We won't get ten feet!" Theodore cried out, astonished the Borini would even suggest such a wild idea. *We'll be lucky to make it two feet!*

"I have a plan." Zilic made his way carefully over to Neup and spoke quietly in his native tongue. Tears glinted in his emerald eyes as he turned to face the children. "You must be brave, my good friends. Listen to what I have to say. Neup and I shall head north, to draw the Massuki away. You must run for the Moritano Mountains. You have to make it."

"No. No, you can't." Minnie could hardly believe what she had just heard. "I won't let you. Zilic, you *can't* do this."

"Please, Zilic," Theodore begged, horrified it had come to this.

"It is the only way. I wish it were otherwise." Zilic climbed into his leather saddle and secured his weapons. "Find the Last Sanctum, Master Reed. You *must* recover the Zeon Stone. Once Neup and I are clear, make for the mountains. Do not look back."

Part 2 • Chapter 9

To friends departed

Salty tears streamed down the sibling's cheeks as Neup and Zilic disappeared into the distance. They felt very much the children they were in that one awful moment. Their legs ached and their lungs burned, but Theodore and Minnie could not stop. Sister and brother ran hand-in-hand over the flattened red clay without a backward glance. Their young hearts throbbed with despair and sorrow.

The Moritano Mountains rose high into the midday sky up ahead, stretching south to north; a confusion of fragmented grey-black rock, with jagged splinters glinting in the sunlight among their rough peaks.

A steep shingle bank littered with broken slate blocks led up and away from the Jetta Deep. The siblings scrambled towards a wide stone ledge running for miles in either direction below the mountains.

"Get further up," Theodore yelled. Clearly, the Massuki could move through sand and clay with ease. He had no desire to find out if they could perform the same trick through the rubble shed from the slopes above.

Minnie slumped down on to the ledge, utterly exhausted. "Do you think... do you think they got away... Neup and Zilic?" She hugged her knees, breathing hard.

Her brother wiped the dust and sweat from his face. "They did." Theodore forced a smile, if only for her. "I feel it. Neup's so quick, they'll never catch him." *Keep him safe, Neup. Run as fast as you can.*

"What do we do until then?"

"Here, have a drink. We'll wait for Zilic."

"What if they don't come back?" *I hate this place,* Minnie thought bitterly. *I hate it.*

"He'll find us." Theodore kept his eyes fixed on the red clay down below. "They'll be here soon, you'll see." *We need you, Zilic. Please come back to us.*

They sat in wait until the late afternoon, willing Neup to appear. Shadows reached down from the mountains as the sun passed slowly overhead, where Eden soared among the cotton clouds. Her silence served as a reassurance that danger—for now—was elsewhere. The siblings were as safe as they could hope to be.

Minnie waved away a hard wedge of bread offered by her brother, even harder now in the heat. Neither had an appetite. Worry and doubt knotted both of their stomachs.

"Maybe they couldn't make it back here," said Theodore. He pointed north. "We should walk along the ledge... that way."

"Do you think it's safe?"

I'm not sure if anywhere here is safe, he thought, but kept it to himself. He eyed the jagged crags and flint shards on the mountainside, breathing in the smell of seared stone in the air. "Well, we can't climb up. It's far too steep." Any attempt to scale the rock-face would end in serious injury. "Come on. It'll be dark soon, and cold. We might find a cave and some wood. We could make a fire to keep us warm."

"Perhaps Zilic would see the fire," said Minnie, feeling the minutest hint of optimism. "The light would show him where we are." The more she thought about the idea, the more appealing it became. A night sitting in the dark offered nothing but misery and gloom.

They quickly emptied the gravel and sand from their pockets, boots, and backpacks, and set off along the ledge, bows and quivers slung over their shoulders. Both looked out over the Jetta Deep along the way, half-expecting a Massuki to burst up from the surface. Minnie shivered as she recalled their awful smell. Mostly, they hoped to see

Neup dashing forward to meet them, with Zilic waving a tiny hand and smiling as they all reunited.

Grit crunched underfoot and wind whistled through the gaps in the rocks like the whispers of unseen phantoms. They were the only sounds to be heard. The children felt uneasy in the shadow of the mountains, as if they were being watched at every step.

"How will we know what to do if we actually find this stupid sanctum?" Minnie asked.

Her brother shrugged. "I hadn't thought that far ahead."

"I wish we had all three stones now, so we could get away from here."

"Me too," Theodore agreed. *Peace in Karadas first, though,* a distant voice hinted. *Those were Legion's words.* "We'll be home before you know it, you'll see." *Well, maybe a little longer than that.*

Minnie smiled. She wanted to believe the words so much. *He's right. It won't be long now.* Hope was all she had left.

The sun vanished behind the mountains. Dusk would come soon. Already, the shadows were growing longer and darker by the minute. The ledge eventually curved sharply to the left, leading into a towering cove, three hundred feet wide at least. Sheer slate walls rose half-a-mile into the sky, split down the centre by a slender crevice as black as coal, as though a monstrous ogre had prised the mountain apart in a fit of rage.

"Perhaps they came here... Zilic and Neup," said Minnie.

"Maybe." Theodore peered around the cove, pulling his cloak tight. "Over there. It looks like trees?"

"Trees and plants," said Minnie. "There must be water here." *Please let there be water.* Even if they were careful, by the next morning their remaining waterskin would run bone dry.

An earthy aroma grew as they approached. It made a welcome change to the dust and sweat they had grown accustomed to. Grey-green shrubs with leaves like swords grew around the crevice, as well as stunted Yucca trees, scorched grass and willowy creepers, clinging to life a stone's throw from the desolate red clay.

"Come and see, Min. It could be a way through."

Minnie peered inside to see a rough staircase leading up into a steep passageway. "It goes straight into the mountains." Pale fungi and tiny mushrooms clung to the crevice walls, soaking up the beads of moisture trickling down the rocks.

"This is it, Min. Dita must have come down this way from the Last Sanctum."

Minnie frowned. "He didn't mention any stairs. I'm not so sure."

Eden screeched up above to startle them both.

The children looked back to see the clay lift and buckle. The surface parted to reveal the black skull of a Massuki, churning through the rock and rubble like a freshly honed plough.

"Get in quick." Theodore grabbed his sister and dragged her inside the passageway. "Up the steps. Go, go, quick."

It was a tight fit. The walls were scarcely a shoulders' width apart. Minnie scrambled forward, only to slip on the damp slate, striking her knees hard against the steps.

Her brother followed close behind until his screams reverberated up the passageway. Churning red cords darted from under the Massuki's skull to snare his ankles. "Get away from me!" A sharp tug pulled him to the ground, dragging him out into the open. "Help, Minnie. Help me!" Theodore clawed at the ground with his dusty fingers, desperate for a notch or chink to grip on to.

Most of the creature's massive frame had now emerged. The Massuki could sense a rare meal was imminent.

It was a struggle for Minnie to even breathe—the creature's rancid stink filled her every breath. She struggled to her feet, reeling in pain, wrestling the bow and quiver from her shoulder. "Leave him alone!"

Vice-like tentacles tugged Theodore further away, twisting up past his knees and digging into his legs. "Minnie… help!" His eyes were wide with horror.

Minnie nocked an arrow, barely able to pull back the string in the space available. *Tsuush*. It was a poor attempt at a strike, closer to skewering her brother than the Massuki. *Come on, you can do this,* she urged herself. *Tsuush.* This one struck closer, but not by much.

An angry groan echoed up the passageway as a third arrow burrowed deep into the creature's black body. The Massuki jerked to one side, slamming its skull against the rock-face.

"Get back, you horrid beast!" Minnie loosed another arrow, and then another, each shaft now finding its target. "Theodore, get up, run!" She charged forward to help her brother back inside the passageway, tugging his wrists and dragging him by an arm.

The Massuki thrashed above and below the ground, shaking the clay surface to a fine powder and sweeping great slate chunks twenty feet to either side. But still it came again, surging forward to smash repeatedly against the entrance, desperate to latch back on to the boy. *Thud. Crunch.* The entire mountain seemed to shake.

"Move, Theo." Minnie slipped again, unbalanced by the unbearable stench.

Slate blocks the size of castle gates came down, shattering into a thousand fragments as they hit the ground. The creature grew ever more furious and frustrated. Its skull was cracked and bloodied by the time it blew an angry snort and slithered beneath the surface in search of easier, less defiant prey.

For a moment, the siblings could only lay there in the dark, breathing deeply and wishing with every thought to be somewhere else.

Minnie's knees and elbow smarted, but her first

concern was for her brother. "Did it hurt you, Theo?"

"Only a little." Theodore laid back on the steps and let out a long huff, massaging some life back into his legs. His face was flushed and sweaty. "Do they *never* give up? I thought that was the end of me."

The children gathered their belongings and shuffled further up the passageway, keen to be away from the Jetta Deep and the relentless Massuki.

"You were splendid with the bow," said Theodore. "Such a brilliant shot."

"I know. I can't believe I got an arrow on target, let alone three!"

"Well, keep it close at hand. We might need it again before too long."

"I hope not." Minnie shivered; half in shock, half with glee.

Twilight came to leave the siblings struggling up a set of steep, twisting stairs in almost complete darkness. The passageway leant at an awkward angle, too, with sharp flint shards jutting from the walls to pull constantly at their clothes and gouge their skin. Before long, their bodies ached.

"At least it's cooler in here," said Minnie, hoping to brighten their spirits. That much was true, at least. After the heat of the red waste, their skin fully welcomed the change.

Thirsty, hungry, and afraid, the children slowed to a halt beside a cramped ledge. Such a dismal perch would immediately be dismissed under normal circumstances. In this hour, though, the ledge made a welcome place to rest their weary limbs. The tantalising gurgle of an underground stream rose up through a gap in the steps to tease their parched mouths.

"I wish our raft had worked," Theodore said dreamily, flexing his back and kneading his jaded hands. "We could be halfway across the ocean by now, almost home. Instead, we're here in a damp hole. A dark, damp, soggy hole."

"So long as we're together." Minnie rubbed her brother's shoulder. She sensed his gloom. She felt it, too. "This *can't* be any worse than living with Aunt Cordelia."

Theodore hadn't thought of their aunt in a while. *Where is she now?* he pondered. He, Minnie, and Cordelia had been en route to New York, to begin a new life, a very different life. While their aunt resumed her duties at a plush boutique in the big city, servicing its unimaginably vain clients, the children had little idea of what to expect. *Would she be thinking of us right now?* He doubted that very much. Out of sight and out of mind would be more in line with her character. *If we ever get back to England, she wouldn't even know. She wouldn't even care.*

"Things will be better in the morning, when the sun comes up," Minnie said, yawning. She rummaged through her pack, hoping to recover a morsel of hidden food. "Here, there's a few berries left. You have them, Theo. You look tired."

He was. He felt utterly drained. The effort and intent to keep the two of them safe had set in. Theodore swallowed his shrivelled berries and promptly fell asleep. Not even the flutter of bats high above or the croaks of a plump brown toad nearby could disturb his deep slumber.

Minnie watched a few stars drift across the gap overhead before she drifted off, too. Visions of their sweet mother and warm-hearted father filled her dreams, back at the cottage where they had all shared a happy life. Playing games in the farmyard with the Downing twins, Ruth and Rosie, skipping among the geese and copper-coloured hens that clucked and pecked at the cobbles. She dreamt of a comfy bed, too, with pillows of spun candy and sheets woven from delicious sugary treats.

Part 2 • Chapter 10

Search for the Sanctum

It was midday when the children awoke, feeling more energised than they had in days. The toad had moved away during the night in search of a less crowded, damp corner. A fresh determination grew as they set out again; an eagerness to find the Last Sanctum and recover the Zeon Stone hidden within, undeterred by what may lurk in the darkness there.

"Come on, Min," Theodore urged. "Maybe Zilic is already at the top. He could have come up this way too."

Minnie followed, desperately trying to flatten her unsightly tangle of red hair. "What about Neup? Would he even fit through here?"

Theodore laughed. "Maybe… if he breathed in a bit!"

"If it gets any tighter, *we'll* have to breathe in too!"

Flint shards glinted like silver knives high up in the walls, caught by the sunlight slanting down into the passageway. The stairs remained as narrow and wearisome as the previous day, but the further they climbed, the wider they became. Even the unpleasant slant in the walls eased, slightly.

"Here, Min, hand me the waterskin." Theodore filled it to the brim from a weak trickle running down a chink in the rocks, while his sister splashed her tanned neck and sunburnt arms with precious liquid.

Minnie screwed up her face partway through a deep gulp. "Yuck! It tastes like rusty nails." Her brother pulled an equally revolted face on sampling the water. They had little choice: suffer the foul, metallic taste, or go thirsty.

"Did you hear that?" Minnie looked around in confusion. "It sounds like Eden."

Theodore tilted his head to see the white hawk peering down into the passageway, squawking meekly. "I see her. Up there." She was barely visible against the narrow strip of cloudy sky high above.

"Eden," Minnie called out. "Stay there. Good girl. We'll be up to you soon."

Another hour went by, struggling up steps so eroded they were more like rounded lumps of gravel and stone. Eventually, the path levelled out and led into a dim, sombre cavern where stalactites hung down like glass ornaments around a crooked opening high in the ceiling. Daylight shone down in a narrow beam to illuminate a brick doorway at the far corner of the cavern. Stone stairs continued on and up through the doorway, but they were entirely out of reach.

"No, no! This isn't fair." Theodore walked forward to stare down into a broad chasm stretching wall to wall; impossible to climb around and far too wide to jump across. This was an obstacle too far. *It can't be!* All the positivity from the morning drained into his feet. Days out in the desert, scorched and thirsty, hunted by the Massuki, not to mention the loss they had endured; all of it now felt entirely in vain. "We'd need *wings* to get over there." Bats burst from the shadows, unsettled by the unusual sound, spiralling around the cave and down into the blackness.

"This can't be happening," Minnie groaned. "There must have been another passage, something we missed."

Her brother looked over at the doorway in the corner, unable to muster any comfort or enthusiasm. "I don't think so. We would have seen it. We'll have to go back down the stairs."

The siblings slumped to the floor, arm in arm, feeling exhausted all over again. The Jetta Deep was a place that neither wanted to ever set eyes on again. Their bodies felt worn; their minds spent. They leant against a wall, sipping gritty, metallic water. It was all they could do. An hour went by in silence before Eden drifted down through the opening, clutching a lifeless shrew in her talons.

Theodore blinked and rubbed at his eyes as the hawk came to rest at the centre of the cavern. He blinked and rubbed his eyes again. *How can that be?* Eden stood preening her snow-white feathers and pecking at her fuzzy treat, perched on nothing but fresh air.

While Minnie sat with her head hung low, picking at the gold trim of her tunic sleeve, her brother gathered up a handful of dirt and tossed it out over the chasm, utterly baffled at the scene. *How is she doing that?* he thought. *She's floating!* The sand and grit disappeared into the blackness below, as expected. But not every grain. A few bits bounced and settled. Eden shrieked, irked that the boy would interrupt her meal.

This is incredible. "Minnie, quick. Come and look." A slender walkway appeared as he swept more grit out into the chasm with his boots. *This is amazing.* "It's a bridge… a hidden bridge!"

"You're acting strange, Theo. What are you doing?" Minnie moved to stand beside her brother with her arms firmly folded.

"It's a way over. Look. Just look."

It took a moment to comprehend the illusion. Her eyes adjusted to see a walkway reaching partway across the chasm, blended perfectly with the backdrop to appear invisible, sculpted long ago by a master stonemason. "What... how did you know?"

"I didn't. It was Eden." Theodore clapped his hands, giddy at his discovery. "Thank *goodness* she arrived when she did. We can get across. I was sure we'd have to turn back."

"You clever girl," said Minnie. The hawk disappeared through the opening in the ceiling to finish her shrew in peace. "It looks awfully narrow. Are you sure it can take our weight?"

Theodore pressed his heel on to the walkway, all the while straining to keep his gaze away from the bottomless drop below, making every effort to mask his own dismay. "If we go slowly, we'll be fine. You weigh less than a feather, anyway."

Even feathers can fall, a voice in her head whispered. "But it only goes half-way. What about the rest of it?"

"That's just where I couldn't reach." Theodore crouched low to fill his pockets with sand and pebbles, adding an extra handful to each for good luck. "Come on. I'll throw down some more as we go. You'll see. The less we think about it, the easier it'll be. We'll be over before you can count to ten."

Minnie took a deep breath and tiptoed out behind her brother, holding up her bow to help balance. *One, two, three,* she counted silently. *Don't look down.* Her heart rose to her throat with each tiny step. *Six, seven... don't look down.*

"See. Nothing to worry about." Theodore's chest thumped as he sprinkled his stockpile of grit to reveal not one, but three separate paths stretching across the void. Each one looked barely the width of his own boots.

Doubt crept into his mind. *Is this a trick? One safe path... and the others set to collapse?* Theodore thought back to the time he and Zilic and Neup had almost perished within the Aradine Mountains. His own blundering had triggered an age-old booby trap to almost bury them alive. All three had escaped, but only just.

"Go on that one," Minnie suggested, pointing to the narrowest of the paths.

"Why that way?"

"It's farthest from the doorway. Most people would take the short path."

It was sketchy logic, but it was all they had to go on. The crunch of sand and stone echoed around the chamber as the siblings inched forward.

"Keep going, Theo." *Eighteen. Nineteen.* Minnie gripped the tail of her brother's cloak, hardly daring to breathe, desperate not to falter. *Twenty-five. Twenty-six.*

The walkway twisted away from the ledge to become even narrower, with the final section an inch in width at most. A last, daring leap delivered the children to the far side.

"We did it. We did it!" her brother laughed. "Maybe our luck is finally changing."

"That wasn't so bad," Minnie lied.

"I think we could be getting closer to the Last Sanctum," said Theodore.

"Really? How do you know?"

"Why else would they hide the bridge?"

Minnie shrugged and hooking her thumbs into her backpack straps. "I suppose." *Anything seems possible in this stupid land,* she thought.

They left through the brick doorway, leaving the chasm and its secret walkway behind. Stairs led up again, chiselled and smooth, a detail not lost on Theodore. "The steps were all worn back there… up the passageway from the desert, I mean. Did you see?"

"So? So what?"

"These look almost brand new."

"So? What are you talking about?"

"*Soooo,* other people must have come up the way we did. But they couldn't get across, so they turned back. No one figured out the puzzle, the hidden bridge." *We did, though. We did.* The thought filled him with fresh hope.

All daylight from the chamber faded as the stairs turned right and then left to leave the children entirely in darkness. Eyes were of no use here. Even with a hand held an inch from her face, Minnie couldn't tell if it was actually there. A damp smell grew as they shuffled on and on, brushing their weathered fingers along the walls of a lengthy corridor.

"I don't like this, Theo."

"Keep going. Follow me." He reached back to take her hand.

It was an hour before their sight returned. A blue haze grew brighter, and round the next corner, tiny lights dotted the walls of a smooth, round tunnel.

"They're snails," Minnie whispered. "Thousands of snails." Her voice echoed along the tunnel as if she had called out. The snails were luminous blue and no larger than a ripe grape, trailing overhead and underfoot to create a cool, welcome glimmer. "They're so pretty." Their eyestalks twitched as she blew gently on to a few of them.

"Pretty *and* helpful. We can actually see where we're going now."

"Don't step on any," Minnie warned. She knew better than anyone how clumsy her brother could be.

The tunnel ran straight before looping up and around in tight, spiralling arcs, like a never-ending corkscrew. Even with the snails' light, their energy soon dwindled. There seemed to be no end to the passageway. Theodore's feet became increasingly cumbersome, too, crunching shells under the flats of his boots, one after the next, much to the dismay of his horrified sister.

A fresh breeze blew along the passageway as they descended a short staircase and turned the corner. The air felt crisp and cool against their skin.

"Can you smell that?" Theodore sniffed the air,

breathing deeply.

Minnie's eyes grew wide at the scent. "It smells like fresh bread." *I'm so hungry I could eat a whole loaf,* she thought. *Maybe two!*

"It does. Bread... and fish, too."

"No! Not more fish." She pinched her nose. "We'll grow scales if we eat any more fish."

"Come on, let's go and see."

"Be careful, Theo. Wait for me."

The snails disappeared from the walls soon after, replaced by the natural daylight shining in through a thick curtain of ivy and vines at the peak of a curving walkway ahead.

Theodore shouldered through the ivy to look along a bright blue reservoir extending a quarter mile to the right, edged with a narrow stone path and enclosed on all sides by towering, craggy walls overspread with bramble and heather. The rugged peaks of the Moritano Mountains reached into the late afternoon sky above, dark bronze in the fading light. "We're here, Min. I think we're actually here." Three waterfalls gushed from on high at the far end of the ravine, from such a great height that the falling water altered to white mist two-thirds of the way down. "Waterfalls. Remember what Dita said about..."

"Theo, look over there." Minnie could scarcely believe her eyes. "Is that...?"

Theodore followed the point of his sister's finger to

see a Borini crouching beside a fire across the reservoir, gently stirring two copper cook pots. Even with his back turned, he instantly recognised Zilic's uncle. "It's Olenious. How on earth did he get here?"

"Olenious!" Minnie yelled.

The Borini spun around, startled by the girl's voice. His face beamed as his eye settled on the children. "Master Reed. Princess, what a joy it is to see you both."

At the same moment, Zilic emerged from the mist below the waterfalls, with Neup scurrying alongside him. The Terap's spirited clicks echoed along the ravine as he spied the youngsters.

"Zilic, you're here! Neup!" Theodore leapt up to punch the air, thrilled to see them both. He and Minnie jogged around the path, leaping over a slot where water gurgled out from the reservoir through a narrow outlet.

The friends reunited beside the fire, hugging and patting Neup's hard shell. It felt wonderful to all be back together.

Zilic bowed low. "It is a relief to see you both alive. We feared the worst for you."

"How did you get away?" Minnie asked, astonished that he and Neup had escaped the Massuki.

"And how did you get here, Olenious?" Theodore added.

"All in good time," he chuckled, tweaking his eye patch. "Let us eat first. Are you both hungry?"

"Famished!" Minnie eyed the cook pots. Her mouth

tingled at the prospect of an actual cooked meal. "It smells wonderful."

The food tasted as good as it smelt. Olenious had prepared a hearty pepper and rabbit stew, delightful sweet nut cakes, and fresh bread twisted on sticks, still warm from the fire. He offered up a fish and mushroom broth, too. Even Minnie couldn't turn her nose up at that. Eden appeared as the friends settled by the fire to polish off any leftovers.

"We almost didn't make it," said Theodore as he ate. "A Massuki attacked us. It nearly got me, too, but Minnie saw it off with her bow. She was incredible."

Zilic smiled and tipped his head to the girl. "So, you *are* a warrior of Karadas after all. As brave and tenacious as our ancestors ever were."

Me, brave? A warrior? Her cheeks glowed. "Do the Borini have girl warriors?"

"We do indeed. It is an honour that all of our people share."

A few stars glimmered through the clouds above the mountains as the world turned dark. Zilic and Theodore packed away the cook pots while Olenious shared the tale of his own journey across the Jurkoon Desert. "Dita was a kind host to me at Valmire," he began. "Once I had learned where you were headed, I followed, only to encounter my nephew and his pursuers."

"We were hunted for miles," Zilic explained. "But while

the Massuki can travel rapidly for a time, thankfully, they are less capable over a longer distance. They gave up the chase after a while. But not without a significant loss."

"What do you mean?" Minnie asked.

"My Terap, Li'cru; the last of the Tri-Horns." Olenious sighed and looked out over the water. "She was not as fortunate as myself. I shall never forget her valour."

"I'm so sorry." Minnie could see the loss of Li'cru etched on his sombre, bronzed face. They sat in silence for a while, fully aware that it could have been any one of them to suffer the same fate as Li'cru.

"Master Reed, we have discovered the Last Sanctum," Zilic announced, keen to lift the mood.

Theodore dropped the copper pot in his hands. "Really? Where is it?"

"Closer than you might think." Olenious pointed his oak staff towards the waterfalls along the ravine, flowing like ribbons of molten silver in the low light.

"How did you get up there?" asked Minnie.

"Lower down. Behind the vapour."

"A perfect shield to disguise the entrance," said Zilic. A shroud of sparkling mist hung at the far end of the reservoir, rising and rolling through the air. "If you are both willing, we shall enter the Last Sanctum at midnight."

Part 2 · Chapter 11

Play the game

The fire had burned down to a circle of ash and embers. Their supplies remained outside beside the reservoir; no need to carry the extra weight. They would be in and out with all haste. That, at least, was the plan.

Theodore hurried along the path to catch up to Zilic. "Did you go inside?" he asked. "Was there anyone in there?" White light from their lanterns caught on the falling mist up ahead, sparkling with all the colours of the rainbow.

"I did not venture past the entrance," Zilic replied. "We shall learn the answer to your second question together."

Silvery swirls of cool vapour brushed over Minnie's

face as she followed the others through to a lofty, hidden hollow beyond the mist. The air there held a wintery touch. Moisture clung to her hair and fingers and clothes, giving rise to a shiver. Her brother shivered, too. Eden remained outside, preferring to keep her feathers dry.

Zilic unfastened a dagger. "This way."

Five broad steps led up and away from the reservoir to reach a tall, peaked doorway edged with coarse flagstones. Only darkness could be seen through the door; a darkness blacker than the night.

"Are you ready, Princess?" Olenious asked, tapping his staff on the top step. "Stay close."

She nodded. *What a cheerless place this is.*

Zilic took the lead and stepped into the gloom. The shadows greedily soaked up the light from their lanterns. Even with all four burning brightly, they could only see a few feet ahead. A narrow slate walkway ran straight, with nothing but blackness above or below.

"Stay close," Olenious said again. "Keep moving."

The gloom remained thick and suffocating as they passed between two immense pillars carved from jagged black rock. A second doorway stood at the end of the walkway, identical to the one at the entrance and equally unwelcoming.

"Wait here," Zilic whispered. His dagger glinting in the lamplight as he disappeared through the doorway. The soft patter of his boots quickly fell silent.

"Be careful," Theodore called after him.

The siblings stood for what felt like an age, straining to see into the darkness beyond the doorway, listening for any hint of the Borini.

"Where is he?" *If I'm a warrior, then why do I feel so afraid?* Minnie asked herself.

Her anxiety eased a little when Zilic returned with a spring in his step. "My friends, I bring good news. The Zeon Stone we seek is truly here."

"Really?" Theodore let out a pent-up breath and excitement swelled in his stomach. "Come on Minnie, we have to see this."

Neup scampered through the doorway behind Zilic and the others followed, edging forward over an uneven slate floor to gather at the centre of a sizeable, circular chamber. Their lanterns shone freely here, no longer strangled by the gloom that dominated the walkway. Blocks of roughly cut stone lay scattered across the floor, and cobwebs hung in sheets from the walls, rising and falling on an unseen breeze like ghostly spirits.

"Careful now," Zilic whispered. A cramped staircase disappeared into the floor a few feet ahead, and two angled doors led off from the chamber, one to the left, the other to the right. But it was the scene immediately ahead that captured their attention. "Neup, stay," he ordered.

The companions placed their lanterns down beside the Terap and shuffled around the staircase.

"The Zeon Stone," Theodore marvelled. *It's really here.* His eyes were fixed on a dusty shaft of light beside the far wall, shining down from a split in the ceiling. A tiny blue sphere gleamed with radiance, suspended in the beam; an enchanting blue, stunning, like the eye of an angel.

"Magnificent," said Olenious.

"It's so bright," Minnie added.

Neup clicked.

"Why is it not guarded?" asked Theodore, mostly to himself. *Surely it can't be this easy?*

Zilic crept forward, scanning the room for any hint of a trap or a pitfall. The first he knew of the invisible barrier up ahead was when his face bumped against it and his dagger clinked.

"What is it?" Theodore called out.

"Impressive." Zilic said under his breath. "It appears to be some kind of protective wall, completely undetectable to the eye." He rubbed a gloved hand against the barrier, brushing one way and then the other in search of an opening. His uncle and Theodore rushed forward to help, but they found nothing, not even a scratch.

"Move aside." Olenious jabbed hard with the butt of his staff, eager to break through to the Zeon Stone. And then again, more forcefully this time. Not only did the barrier fail to break, each strike made hardly a sound.

"Welcome, welcome," a sinister, well-spoken voice announced. "Why, it's been so very long since I had a visitor here."

Theodore stumbled back, startled and spooked. A smooth stone slab rose into the ceiling to reveal a doorway behind the Zeon Stone, and a remarkable creature slithered out on a fat tail coated in violet scales. While its lower body was clearly that of a serpent, a thin upper body, arms, and overly swollen head looked to be more human in form, with shoulder and rib bones pushing against the pale skin of its freckled torso.

"Who are you?" Zilic crouched low with his daggers poised.

"I think I shall ask the questions," the creature snapped back. Its tail quivered threateningly. "Tell me. Why are you here?" The man-snake glared at each of his visitors in turn through the joyless yellow eyes of a demon. Scraggy, pointed ears only helped to reinforce the image. "In fact, do not bother. There is no need. Obviously, you have come here for this." He circled the light beam, gazing at the Zeon Stone. "I'm afraid that cannot be. The Keeper cannot allow that."

"May we trade with you for the stone?" Olenious asked. "It is important we acquire it."

The Keeper smiled. "Important? Why did you not say so earlier? By all means, it is yours. *Please,* help yourself." His smile turned to a grimace, and then vanished.

The friends took a step back as a fine green mist rolled over the floor, evaporating after a few moments to reveal an oval pit at their feet, filled with bones and skulls, rusted chain mail and steel helms, swords, shields, armour, and scraps of cloth and leather.

"May I introduce you to my previous visitors," said the man-snake.

Minnie reached for her brother's hand, unnerved at the gruesome tomb laid before them.

"The Guardian, Legion, he sent us," Theodore said timidly.

"Excellent try, my young friend." A manacle at the Keeper's wrist jangled as he waved a hand dismissively. "But the Zell-Ku are no more. Gone forever."

"They're not," cried Minnie. "My brother isn't lying."

The Keeper looked around with a mock expression of fear on his face. "No, please don't tell them I'm here. *Please* don't." The grimace returned. "I found this place. I liked it, so I stayed. I keep order here now. The Last Sanctum is mine. Do you deny me?"

"We do," Olenious growled. "We deny you with every breath."

Zilic tapped his daggers together. *Clink, clink.* "Move aside, Keeper, and we shall spare you."

"You have nothing to threaten me with," he shrieked. "Nothing!" The man-snake placed a scrawny hand against the invisible barrier and peered down into the pit. "If these fine specimens failed to break through, what hope would a tiny speck like you have?"

They could not oppose the truth of his words. Even with his most vigorous strike, Olenious had made no impact at all on the barrier. For now, their host remained entirely safe, a fact he seemed to know all too well.

"We don't seem to be getting along, do we?" the Keeper groaned, inspecting his filthy, cracked fingernails. "I know. How about we play a game? A *fun* game. Do you like games? If you win, the Zeon Stone is yours."

"And if we lose?" asked Zilic.

The man-snake gestured down to the armour and bones. "If you lose, well, then you get to stay here forever, with my previous guests."

Olenious bristled, furious they were being made fools of. "What are the rules to this… this game?"

"Simple. You must choose a path." said the Keeper. He pointed to the doorways on either side of the chamber. "Or take the stairs if you wish. Find a way to the stone, and I shall let you keep it."

They retreated a few paces to consider his peculiar offer.

"It *must* be a trap," Theodore whispered. *It must be.*

"We have little choice," Olenious said. "Let me go alone."

"No one will go alone," said Zilic, nodding to Minnie. "Either we all play this so-called game, or we leave now, empty-handed." He turned to face the Keeper. "We accept this challenge. But I warn you, be true to your word, or you shall not find us so agreeable."

"Now, now, there's no need for threats. My word is my

honour. I would *never* deceive you. Never."

"Uncle, take Neup and check the doorways. We shall explore the stairs."

Olenious swept up a lantern and vaulted up into Neup's saddle. "Stay alert, Zilicarillion, and keep my friends safe." With that, he ushered the Terap through the doorway to the left to begin their search.

The man-snake spoke in an almost pleasant tone as Zilic moved to retrieve his own lantern. "Oh, you shall not need that, my tiny friend. I have provided ample light to guide you."

"A kind offer," Zilic muttered. "But one we must decline."

"I have to insist." The Keeper slithered back through the doorway, rattling his tail. "It is written in the rules."

Theodore paced nervously. "Please, Zilic, can we just get this over with?"

"Very well." Grudgingly, the Borini left the lanterns where they lay and led the children over to the stairwell. They descended into the gloom to arrive at a large, crumbling ledge, holding their breath to block out a stale whiff in the air.

The darkness melted away as a dozen oil lamps burst to life, and then a dozen more. A hundred orange flames soon burned brightly throughout an enormous cavern, where narrow walkways and stone stairs, timber ladders and rope and chain bridges stretched up above and deep below, as far as their eyes could see.

"Where do we even begin?" said Minnie, overwhelmed by the impossible maze laid out before them.

"Begin at the beginning." The Keeper's voice echoed around the chamber. "Choose swiftly, though. My lamps will not burn forever." To illustrate his point, every flame throughout the cavern dwindled a touch.

An iron gate lowered from the ceiling behind them, too, clanging against the floor to expel any thoughts of a retreat. Alarm altered to panic. Thoughts of being trapped within a labyrinth were unpleasant; to be here, fumbling in the darkness, would be utterly terrifying.

Zilic rubbed his palms together, trying to figure out a logical path to the Zeon Stone. "The stairs led down, which would suggest that the exit is above us."

"So we go up then," said Theodore.

Minnie peered out over the ledge. "Maybe we go down first," she suggested. "It can't be that simple, Theo, to just go up?" *That wouldn't be much of a game,* she thought.

"This is true," Zilic agreed. He turned to Theodore and said, "Perhaps we must step back to go forward."

He remained unconvinced, but they had him outvoted. "Which way, then?" Theodore huffed.

To their left and ahead, narrow steps led up to a wooden platform suspended on thick, knotted ropes, and a ladder to the right led down. Theodore and Minnie followed Zilic down the ladder to reach a rocky mantel below. From here, another two ladders hung down, while a sandy walkway lay across the gap ahead.

"How about that one?" Minnie suggested.

Again, they went down, choosing the ladder to their left this time. With every obstacle overcome, the oil lamps faded a little more to heighten their dilemma. Five more ladders and a curving staircase followed, then a lengthy rope bridge leading up to a craggy stone column. The friends tiptoed down a set of spiral stairs carved into the column and over several timber beams that bowed under their weight, along walkways and down stone steps, up ladders and across a precarious swing bridge that felt seconds from falling apart beneath their boots.

Minutes turned to hours, and they were still no closer to finding the exit. Every step became ever more perilous as the lamps gave out one after the next, until barely a quarter remained alight, leaving much of the cavern hidden in shadow.

"This is hopeless," Theodore groaned, wishing they had climbed up from the very beginning. "We'll never get out of here."

A tail rattle and sneering laughter drifted down from above.

The oil lamp beside Minnie spluttered and perished. "He's enjoying this," she cried out. Tears welled in her eyes. Once the last light disappeared, tears would be all her eyes would be good for. "It's all been a stupid trick... just to trap us in here."

Theodore huffed and hurled his backpack to the floor, overcome with frustration. "I don't like this game." He slumped against a timber upright and held his head in his hands. "We can't win. We can't even see where we're going!"

It was his sister that noticed the pale light spilling out across the floor, twinkling in the deepening gloom. "Wait. Theo, look." Minnie pointed to his backpack.

Her brother scrambled forward, tearing open the drawstrings. The glow grew to a gleam as he reached inside to pull the Dagger of Shard out into the open. "Look at this, Zilic." The light faded as Theodore turned towards the Borini, but returned when he faced up to his sister.

"Turn back towards me, Master Reed," said Zilic. And so he did. The crystal blade immediately lost its sheen, just as it had before. "Good, now circle around, slowly."

Minnie watched on, transfixed, as her brother turned one way and then the other. With every movement, the dagger altered from light to dark.

"Very good," said Zilic, leading the boy to a timber walkway behind them. "Direct the weapon this way." The blade gleamed a little more.

Theodore laughed, and his body swelled with excitement. He rushed forward to seek a way through the maze. "It's showing us the way. Come on." The glow dimmed as he turned to the right, but shone brighter than ever up ahead.

"Try here," said Minnie.

On and up they went, guided by the light of the dagger, around curving sandy steps, over a rusted chain bridge, and up more ladders than any of them cared to count, on and on and on until their legs and arms ached.

Theodore gasped as they came to a wooden platform studded with iron tacks high up in the cavern. "We did it," he whispered. "Minnie, we did it." He jogged forward, squinting into the shadows beyond, delighted to see the exit up ahead and the unmistakable blue sparkle of the Zeon Stone through the doorway, suspended in the light beam. Delight quickly altered to frustration when he almost toppled head first over the edge of the platform and into a dark chasm; a chasm growing darker by the second as the oil lamps all around snuffed out one by one.

"A valiant effort, my friends." The Keeper slunk from the exit and out on to a wide stone ledge opposite, clapping two scrawny hands. "A valiant effort indeed." A timber drawbridge hanging down below the ledge quivered as he casually brushed the dust from an operating lever set in the wall. The drawbridge rose an inch or two, but no more.

"We played your game," Theodore yelled. "Raise the bridge. We won."

"You found a way through," the Keeper admitted. His face held a sullen look. "That much is true. But not without cheating!"

Minnie's face turned red with fury. "Cheating? How dare you say that!"

"In what way have we been dishonest?" Zilic asked calmly.

The man-snake pointed at the dagger in Theodore's hands. "With that," he snarled. "You were *supposed* to use your wits!"

Zilic remained composed. "We did as you asked. The game is over."

"Very well, my tiny friend," he muttered, forcing a black smile. His yellow eyes closed, and the Keeper calmed himself with a deep breath. "I agree. The game *is* over."

"Thank you," Minnie called over the void.

A vile snigger echoed around the cavern. "The game is over, and it is you who lose. None of you shall ever leave the Last Sanctum."

Theodore felt sick to the pit of his stomach. He reached for his sister's hand, listening to the laughter and watching the last of the oil lamps fade to specks of orange flame.

Part 2 • Chapter 12

Deceitful Schemes

"Raise the bridge," Theodore screamed. *You horrid, spiteful creature.*

The Keeper turned away, humming tunelessly to himself. "If you cannot play fair, then you must remain here. These were the rules." He moved towards the doorway. "Rules *must* be followed. Have no fear, though. I shall return… someday… to collect your bones."

"No, no, you can't," Minnie begged. "Please, don't leave us here."

Theodore's anger flared. He passed the Dagger of Shard to his sister and set an arrow to his bow. *Tsuush.* The arrow flew across the chasm, only to ricochet off an invisible shield and tumble uselessly into the pitch blackness below.

"It can't be," said Minnie, hugging herself. "Another barrier. He's trapped us in here." Even if they could raise the drawbridge, she knew there was no way to break through.

Her brother fired again, and again the arrow sprang back. *Ping.*

"That wasn't very pleasant," the man-snake sneered. "Is this how you repay my goodwill?"

"Keeper," Zilic called over. "Are you aware of what this is?" Thinking fast, he snatched the dagger from Minnie's hand.

"What are you doing?" Theodore gasped.

Zilic gave a discreet wink. "Have you not heard of the Dagger of Shard? This blade is the most powerful weapon in all of Karadas."

The Keeper hid his intrigue well, but not that well. A nervous tail rattle confirmed his curiosity. "Speak."

"Allow us safe passage from the Last Sanctum, and the Dagger of Shard shall be yours."

He shrugged his bony shoulders. "And *why* would I do that? There is no need. The blade is already mine. In time, I shall pluck it from your lifeless hand. You have no food and you have no water. How long do you think to survive in here?"

As much as Zilic and the children hated the situation,

it was a valid point. With patience—once the companions had taken their last breath—they would be powerless in keeping the dagger from his grasp. But the Keeper was far from patient; why wait for days to pass when he could claim the Dagger of Shard immediately?

"Very well. I feel in a generous mood today. Lay down your weapons and step back. When I lower my shield, cast the blade over, and I shall allow you to leave."

"You can't let him have it!" Theodore screamed. He held up both hands and moved to stand between the Borini and the chasm. "He'll cheat us, I know it."

"Stand aside, boy," the man-snake ordered, angry at the boy's meddling, already infatuated with possessing the dagger.

Zilic winked again, more obviously this time. "Trust me," he whispered. "He seems to like games. Let him play mine."

The companions set their bows down and stepped back.

"A little further. That's it, another step." His yellow eyes narrowed. Once satisfied that his guests posed no further threat, the Keeper raised the flats of his hands in the air. His swollen head quivered, straining to manipulate the invisible barrier with whatever strange sorcery held it in place.

"Are you ready?" asked Zilic.

The man-snake gave a nod, eyeing the Borini for any hint of betrayal. Time stood still as the Dagger of Shard spun leisurely through the air, much to the displeasure of the Keeper, who had been expecting a more straightforward catch.

Zilic rolled forward in a heartbeat and nocked an arrow to his bow. *Tsuush.* A loud twang rang around the cavern as the arrow sliced through the counterweight rope holding the drawbridge down. "Look out!" The rope frayed and tore apart.

A hefty sack of gravel fell from high above to smash on to the platform, inches from where Minnie stood. She dived to one side as the bridge rose promptly, thumping hard against the platform with a deep boom.

"Deceiver!" The Keeper dithered for a second too long, torn between seizing the dagger and raising his protective shield. He chose the former, to his detriment.

All three were over the bridge and on to the opposite ledge in seconds, surrounding the Keeper with their bows raised high. The creature clasped the crystal blade against his underfed body, sobbing and trembling. "Please," he begged, "please do not harm me... please!"

"You lose." Theodore plucked the dagger from his feeble grip and returned it to his backpack.

"Now, I think we shall play a new game," said Zilic. He lowered his bow and backed through the doorway to stand beside the light beam. "We will leave here, and the stone shall leave with us."

"Yes... yes," the Keeper stuttered. "A *wonderful* idea, an excellent game."

Minnie kept an arrow aimed at the sniffling creature

as she and her brother joined Zilic, marvelling at the Zeon Stone; a magical orb of complete perfection. They had only to reach out, and the treasure would be theirs.

"Such a pretty thing," said the man-snake. "Please, yes… you must take your prize."

"Go on, Theo, we've earned this," Minnie urged.

Tiny white flares danced on the stone's surface as Theodore reached into the light beam with a trembling hand. Four fingers curled gently around the stone, and a thumb over the fingers. It held a fiery heat and an icy bite in the same moment, though not at all painful. "We did it," he whispered. "We actually did it."

The light beam crackled and vanished, and the invisible barrier at their back dissolved into a shower of grey flakes.

Laughter filled the Last Sanctum. "You simple-minded boy!" the Keeper screamed through the doorway. His false tears were already dry. "You have sealed your own fate. Without the words, you have cursed the stone."

Minnie pulled her bow string tight. "What do you mean?"

"Did your *precious* Guardian not explain?"

"What words?" Doubt and foreboding swelled inside Theodore's chest, and a chill crept down his neck. "What words?"

"The incantation… words that release the stone. Even I would not be fool enough to remove it without speaking the incantation."

Theodore felt sick. "You're lying." *There were no words,* he thought, frantically trying to recall his exchange with the Guardian. There was no recollection of an incantation, however, only Rakista laying siege to the plateau, casting Legion down to the ocean before he could impart his knowledge fully.

"Believe me, or do not. I may be the overseer of the stone, but I am certainly not its champion." A cruel grin spread over the Keeper's face, and he sniggered. "I look forward to you meeting him." He yanked down hard on a chain and the stone door between the chambers gradually lowered to the floor. "Before we part ways, I must ask, have any of you ever encountered a titan?"

Zilic hadn't. The siblings certainly hadn't.

"His name… is Nylos, the Titan of the Last Sanctum. He will not cease in his hunt for the prize you have *stolen.* Nylos shall be the ruin of you, the ruin of all of Karada…"

The door thumped against the floor with a low rumble, cutting off the Keeper's venomous words.

Part 2 · Chapter 13

Dark Liberation

The bow in Minnie's hand trembled and her head throbbed, unable to make sense of what was happening. "Who's Nylos?" she asked.

Zilic shook his head. "It is not a name I am familiar with."

"Can we please just go?" Theodore squeezed the Zeon Stone tightly in his palm. *He's fibbing,* he thought angrily. *Just because we won, and he lost.*

Neup arrived back into the chamber, skidding to a halt beside the children. "Zilicarillion!" Olenious called out from his saddle. "I looked everywhere. You were gone for so long. Where did you go?"

Minnie glared at the stairwell. "He trapped us down there."

"Neup and I could find no way through to the stone," Olenious went on. "This entire place is a mystifying web of confusion. We discovered a passageway leading down into the mountain, an enormous passageway, with steps twice the height of Galenta's great feasting hall. It is unlike anything I have ever..."

"We have it, Olenious," Theodore blurted, keen to report on their success. "We have the Zeon Stone, look." Radiant blue light streamed between his fingers as he opened his hand.

But before any of them could savour the moment, the Last Sanctum shuddered violently. The walls fractured, and the floor trembled. Spurts of sand and grit trickled down from the ceiling high above.

"What's happening?" Minnie yelled. She watched on in horror as the doorway leading back out to the ravine crumbled before her eyes. The frame and heavy stone lintel caved in to bury the entrance, followed quickly by the doorway heading off to the left. "How do we get out now?"

The entire room began to break apart. Dust rose in choking grey clouds and slabs the size of barn doors detached from the walls to crash against the floor.

"Through there," Olenious called out, wrestling to keep Neup under control. "Go now. Run!"

Only the doorway to the right remained. The children

sprinted behind Neup, leaping over cracks and weaving between the falling rocks. Even with their arms held overhead, a single blow would be fatal. Zilic came last, darting head first through the doorway, seconds before the entire chamber vanished under the weight of the mountains above. On and on they fled through a network of lamp-lit corridors, twisting left and then right to arrive at a dead end.

"There's no way out." Theodore's face turned pale. *We're trapped.*

Olenious gave no reply. He leapt down and shuffled through a duct just above the floor. "We are close. Follow me." Tiles around the opening fell away and shattered as Neup squeezed inside, almost too large to fit through. Groans from the ceiling urged the others to follow.

"Keep moving," Theodore screamed. He tucked the Zeon Stone into a pocket and crawled in behind his sister, scuffing his knees and elbows against the coarse stone. "Go faster. Move!"

Zilic and the siblings spilled out into a dank, sandy chamber that felt ready to come apart at any moment. Part of the ceiling had already collapsed. Water gushed in from above, spraying down on to the mounds of flint and sand below.

"No. No, it can't be!" Olenious charged into a circular tunnel up ahead, crashing against a stout timber lattice with his shoulder. "The gate. It wasn't here before." He rattled it with all of his strength, but the gate stood firm. Even as Neup slashed at the barrier, snaring a mandible in the mesh, the gate would not yield.

Minnie sank to her knees, whispering into her hands. "We should never have come here."

"There must be another way?" said Theodore. His voice could barely be heard above the rumbling water and the grind of shifting rock. He looked at the Borini with wide, frightened eyes. "There has to be?"

"I have an idea." Zilic slipped back through the duct and returned with a pair of small ceramic oil lamps, leaning them deliberately against the gate.

His uncle gave a knowing nod. "My friends, step away. Take cover."

Theodore and Minnie scampered back as far as they could to watch Zilic nock two arrows. He quickly drew back his bowstring and released. *Whoosh.* The oil lamps erupted into a fireball as the arrows struck; a fireball far larger than expected. Fearsome heat, rolling flames, and thick black smoke surged along the tunnel with an angry roar. It took a minute or more, but once the fire died down and the fumes dispersed, only a curtain of ash and charred sticks remained where the gate had stood.

"You did it!" Minnie cheered. The plan had worked perfectly. Neup rushed forward to sweep the lingering debris aside.

The friends raced through the blackened tunnel,

struggling to balance as the surrounding rock juddered and splintered. Four tall pillars stood at the end of the passageway, where water vapour wafted in from the waterfalls beyond.

Minnie squeezed between the pillars, peering thirty feet down to the reservoir below. "We're nearly out," she yelled, wiping the moisture from her face. "We're behind the waterfalls... just above the entrance."

"How do we get down?" Theodore cried.

Olenious shuffled forward to look out. "We must jump to the water."

It was the answer he had dreaded. "Jump? From here?" *This is madness,* he told himself. *We're too high up.*

The tunnel buckled and a wedge of the slate crashed to the ground an inch behind Minnie's legs. Another fell, larger than the first. "You have to, Theo," she said firmly. "We can't stay here."

"Swim away as soon as you can," said Zilic, securing his bow. "Get clear. This entire place may come down on top of us."

Minnie went first. She drew in a sharp breath and stepped forward, with her hair and cloak flapping madly as she dropped. Olenious and Neup followed, splashing into the reservoir to send plumes of frothing water firing into the air.

"I shall be with you all the way," Zilic said calmly. He and the boy jumped together.

It took a second to reach the water, but to Theodore, it felt like a lifetime. His screams fell silent as he thumped against the surface, hitting the water with a painful slap to force the breath from his lungs.

Jagged rocks and splintered timber beams rained down through the mist from where they had escaped. *Crash. Splash.* The friends were far from safe.

Theodore and Minnie thrashed at the water, weighed down by clothing and weapons, gulping desperately for air. When a deep groan vibrated throughout the ravine, the panic truly set in.

"Go!" Olenious cried out, coughing violently. "Move!"

It came down like an avalanche through the darkness. As if in slow motion, the entire cliff face collapsed like butter sliding from a hot knife. A million tons of shattered rock smashed into the reservoir behind them with a monumental boom, louder than a hundred mighty thunder storms. Then came the surge. The water rose up as if it were alive, sweeping forward to lift the companions into the air and drag them along the ravine. The wave reached the far wall to break against the rocks in an eruption of white water.

"Hold on," Theodore screamed. "Minnie!" Foaming waves swirled all around, stinging his eyes. He clung hopelessly to his sister, struggling to keep above the surface, grasping at the heather and roots sprouting between the rocks.

Minnie held on with all the strength left in her arms, wrapped around her brother's waist, spluttering and coughing.

Eventually, the water rolled back and forth, and finally settled.

"Min... are you all right?" *That was worse than awful!*

His sister held up a thumb and swept the hair away from her face. *That was so exciting!*

The siblings clambered down to a rock mantle, ten feet up from the reservoir. They slumped against the wall, breathing hard, utterly astounded at their survival.

"My friends, are you safe?" Olenious called out. He and Zilic floundered upon a ledge a little further down, wrestling to untangle one another from a bramble bush, and plucking thorns from their palms.

"I think so," Theodore called back. *I don't know how!*

"We're safe," Minnie shouted down. "We're safe."

Neup emerged from the water, clicking and shaking the water from his glossy shell further along the wall.

"Do you need any assistance?" asked Zilic.

"Wait there. We'll come down to you."

Theodore and Minnie made their way down in the dark, taking great care not to slip. They nudged past roots and sharp stones that grasped at their skin and clothes. By the time they were all reunited, the reservoir had drained a few feet more, sloshing and gurgling through the narrow outlet at the far end of the ravine.

"Look at that," said Theodore. He looked back to where the three waterfalls had flowed only a short time ago. Only a crumbled rock face remained now, illuminated by a low half-moon. Water streamed down through a hundred newly formed cracks and splits, gushing around clean-cut stones and drifts of dust and gravel.

"That wasn't so difficult," Olenious chortled, wringing the moisture from his cloak. "One Zeon Stone down, two more to go."

Zilic folded his arms and raised an eyebrow.

"The stone!" Theodore's body tensed. He clawed at his tunic pocket and let out a long, thankful breath. *I still have it.* Blue light glimmered between his thumb and forefinger as he drew the Zeon Stone out into the open. "We did it, Minnie. We actually did it." He flicked the hair from his eyes and smiled.

"Does this mean we can go home soon?" It was all she wanted; to return to Corsham, back to a normal life. Asleep or awake, she thought of little else. Minnie leant back against the heather to gaze at the Zeon Stone, hypnotised by its effortless beauty.

A deafening crack brought a swift end to her daydream.

She and her brother leapt to their feet, staring at the newly formed cliff face—where the Last Sanctum had remained a secret for so very long. An enormous slate slab fell forward, clattering on to the rubble piled up below. *Crash.* A second block tumbled. *Smash.* And then another. *Thud.*

Zilic moved along the ledge, gazing into the shadows. "Something's breaking out," he muttered to himself. His mouth fell open as a colossal blunted arm appeared through the breach, swiping away the last stone blocks that had served as a prison wall up until now. Water streamed down from above, turning immediately to vapour on contact with the glistening black limb. Steam hissed angrily, pouring out from the opening.

Minnie gaped with unbelieving eyes. "It's a giant!" she breathed. *This can't be real.* "A giant made of stone."

"Not a giant," Zilic corrected her. "Nylos."

"The *Titan?*" Theodore shivered from head to toe. "The Keeper... the man-snake, he warned us. Why didn't we listen?"

Only a hazy silhouette of the creature could be seen within the rock-face, doused by the moonlight and shrouded in steam, but even so, Nylos made for an unimaginable sight: two hundred feet of immortal dread, an unbreakable demigod forged from jet-black obsidian and ancient, dark wizardry. A red blaze burst to life within the Titan's featureless face like a great fiery eye, illuminating a tall, cylindrical head crowned in jagged shards above broad, black shoulders.

The children shrunk back into the heather, horrified at the sight. Goosebumps rose over their skin and their blood turned to ice, watching liquid rock and glass bubble and ooze from the Titan's eye, seeping down in orange globules to hiss and fizz upon his hulking chest.

"We didn't know," said Minnie. "We weren't told about him."

Theodore reached for her hand, silently pleading to awaken from this darkest of dreams. *Legion, why didn't you tell me the words, the incantation?* "He should have told me," he whispered. "What in all the world have we done?"

With a monstrous, creaking stride, the Titan emerged fully.

Minnie and Theodore's adventures will continue in

A darkness hangs over the realm.
The siblings remain in mortal danger, facing daunting pitfalls and hostility at every turn. But they're not finished yet.
Can Minnie and Theodore somehow help to liberate Karadas?
Will the pair realise their dream of ever returning home?

Expect surprises and a whole heap of jeopardy!

Available in print and digital formats soon.

Spectre of Destiny

Thank you so much for choosing
to read Spectre of Destiny.

Have you enjoyed this book?

If you did, please take a moment to leave a short
review on Amazon, Goodreads, or wherever
you purchased your copy.

About the author
J. T. Mather

James lives in Nottinghamshire, UK.
Karadas: The Veiled Realm, Spectre of Destiny is
his debut young adult fantasy adventure story.

Currently, he is working on the sequel to Spectre of Destiny,
while also developing a mind-boggling sci-fi adventure.
Watch this space!

He enjoys exploring the countryside with his partner, son,
and siblings, as well as playing tennis, football, and crazy golf.
Oh, and James has a curious fascination with insects!
His latest, compulsive viewing includes Arcane; an
incredible animated series set in the realm of Runetera.
"Quite stunning. A must watch." ★★★★★

Check out James's website for links to social media and to learn
more about the movies, books, and more, that helped inspire the
creation of an entire fantasy world—Karadas—using nothing
but his imagination (and a few chocolate biscuits).

www.jtmather.com

Maybe you'll be inspired to pick up a pen
and start creating your own unique world!

Acknowledgments

I couldn't have accomplished my publishing dream without your support. Thank you all so much.

Vicki Mum Sam

Shae Sue Tamsin

David Chris Matt

Jerome Roisin Alex

Alison Sylva

Rebecca Simon Frances

In memory of

Paul Mather 1944 - 2021

Love you Dad.

Food for thought...

- What did you like best about the story?
- Who were your favourite characters?
- If you were Minnie or Theodore, what would you have done differently?
- How important was the time period to the story?
- Which area of Karadas would you most like to visit and why?
- What was your favourite chapter?
- Which creature would you least like to meet?
- What surprised you most about the book?
- If Spectre of Destiny was made into a movie, who would you like to see cast as the lead characters?
- If you had the chance to ask the author one question, what would that question be?
- What should happen next in the story, and can all the main characters survive until the end?

CPSIA information can be obtained
at www.ICGtesting.com
Printed in the USA
LVHW080106270522
719855LV00004B/5